# Seventeen

Scott Richards

Published by Scott Richards, 2018.

SEVENTEEN

**First edition. September 28, 2018.**



ISBN: 978-1719897242

Written by Scott Richards.

# Chapter One

I can hear her in the cellar; struggling, squirming on a chair. Lines of fresh blood trickle to drip inexorably from open wounds on her wrists. The self-inflicted damage and pain caused by cable ties chafing, and digging into captive flesh; tearing, shredding tender young meat.

If I switch on a monitor in the lounge, I can watch her twitching, panic evident in wide eyes, constantly hunting the room, occasionally fixing on steps leading up to the cellar door. I'm amazed by the quality of infra-red images from cameras I installed, even though they're only black and white.

Pretty soon, I'm going to have to accept the fact I've reached a point of no return; the moment when I know for certain there can be no going back, and only one realistic outcome to this situation. She knows it too. She can sense her impending mortality.

It's her own fault. Well, that's what I've been telling myself for the past twenty-four hours and, when I'm truly reconciled to that, then I'll also have the courage to end it, once and for all. The hole in the garden is deep enough, and I've plenty of plastic pond liner.

My only concern is if the knuckle-dragging boyfriend comes snooping around, or, worse still, the police. I don't want plod poking, probing; sticking their unwanted beaks into my business. They should have done that in the first place, when the shit kicked off, and I reported them. As usual though, they've more pressing matters to attend to; racing around like Starsky and fucking Hutch in squad cars, chasing speeding motorists in stolen cars, picking up drunkards in city centre precincts, or pushing unwanted flyers through my letterbox, informing me about the rapid increase of burglary in the area. The cheeky bastards even had the audacity to tell me that the locks on my doors are sub-standard.

Well, as far as I'm concerned, if they're good enough to keep a bunch of nosey coppers out of my business, then the locks are fine with me.

She's fidgeting around again, trying to make herself comfortable, or as comfortable as she could be, under the circumstances. I can hear chair legs scraping on the stone floor, as she mewls and wails, even with a length of duct tape stretched over her mouth.

I'll mute the sound from the intercom, put on a bit of music, or maybe watch the BBC's six o'clock news.

No, on second thoughts, I'll listen to music, because if I watch the news, I'll get angry. I'll find something on there to annoy or infuriate me, to the point where I'll act irresponsibly or regrettably. I must stay calm and rational, and remain in control. *Watermark* by Enya should do the trick. It usually relaxes me, lets my mind drift freely on an ocean of soothing lilting melodies.

I'm standing at a kitchen worktop, by a window near the sink, listening to the rasp of honing steel, as it slides effortlessly along the blade of the knife, and *Miss Clare Remembers.*

As *Evening Falls* plays, darkness engulfs the garden. I see my reflection in the glass; all wrinkles and grey hair, blue eyes fixed, hypnotic, lips pressed into a determined line. There's a fine halo of stubble on my face. I really do need a shave, but I'll do it later when I shower; afterward.

Then I realise I'll need a hacksaw from the shed, and I'll have to replace the blade. A bi-metal, thirty-two teeth per inch, is probably the best to use. I'm fairly sure that the hardened blade will cut though bone without too much trouble or effort. It will definitely be quieter than using a portable hand-grinder, and no spatter either.

I grab a torch from the airing cupboard, check that the battery is okay, and then unlock the back door. Cool air wafts in as I step onto concrete paving, meandering in a sinuous serpentine trail to the shed, skirting around the mound of fresh excavation, and roll of pond liner. I let the beam play around the pit's perimeter for a moment, as my mind calculates, re-checking the depth.

The shed door creaks on rusted hinges as it opens, startled moths flutter around my head, drawn to the beam in wild zigzag patterns as I pluck a saw from the rusty nail where it hangs, glittering invitingly.

I grab a new blade from the toolbox under the bench, and return to the house. I recite my mantra. A definition of the point of no return; the stage at which it is no longer possible to stop what you are doing, and when its effects cannot now be avoided or prevented.

Yes, I think that sums it up in a nutshell.

What's coming cannot be avoided or prevented.

Definitely not.

# Chapter Two

I've lived on Longridge Crescent for thirty-two years. I moved here just after my daughter, Lizabeth, was born in eighty-eight, when the local manufacturing industry was in decline, when Thatcher was at the helm, clinging to her throne, but when mortgages were easier to secure.

Remember those halcyon days?

We didn't need to save for a deposit then.

The building society set us up with a hundred percent mortgage, attached to an endowment policy. Of course, at the time, we didn't know we were being sold a fucking pup, or that interest rates were about to rocket to a record high or that repaying interest on the capital we borrowed would financially cripple us on a monthly basis.

Still, you live and you learn, don't you?

That's what they say these days, isn't it?

Well, we lived, and we learned all right. We learned to scrape by on a pittance, to keep a roof over our heads - just - and to keep the wolf from the door, which is funny, really; ironic after the last few months, to be honest.

Even-numbered houses are on the longer, outer curve of the Cres, as most residents call it, and odd-numbered on the shorter curve. The Cres is on an incline, and higher numbered houses are at the top of the slope, the lower at the bottom. My house is near the bottom, before a bend. Gardens at the back of the evens are much bigger than the odds, because odd numbers back onto Badger Close and, under present circumstances, my larger, private space is proving ideal. No neighbours to see anything, or report anything to anyone.

I live at number twenty-four, which my wife, Selena, God rest her soul, set her heart on the moment it went on the market. Her eldest brother, Jonathon, lived next-door-but-one at number twenty-eight for five years. Then he set up a plant nursery business in Lincolnshire, and moved.

If I remember rightly, his wife Gina was diagnosed as having a massive brain tumour not long after they left; a messy affair that was too.

Her health nose-dived rapidly, the nursery and plants were neglected, ruined, leaving them facing bankruptcy. He put one barrel of his shotgun to her head, blew the tumour, and her brains, onto the wall, and put its twin to his chin about thirty seconds after. Selena took a long time to get over the shock, as did most of her family.

I was stunned but, to be honest, I have to admit that I always thought Jonathon was a bit of a nutter, although in his defence, he's the only one of her four brothers I could have a conversation with, or anything in common with. It was mostly about medication; antidepressants and such, or the odd gardening tip.

I always refer to her side of the family as the Outlaws rather than the in-laws, and I'm always keen to point out to anyone who'll listen that you can choose your friends, but you can't choose your family. I'm pretty much stuck with the bastards, not that I see them very often now that Selena's dead and buried. She was actually cremated, and her ashes scattered on a memorial plot at the front of the house; only a small garden, tastefully planted with shrubs and perennials, or it used to be.

Mark, the youngest of the clan, is an abrasive bastard, and such a condescending little shit, too. Robert's a smug fucker, and Michael, the eldest? Well, Michael's one of those twats who, when you ask him how he is, you'll wish you hadn't. He's a hypochondriac, with a list of fucking ailments as long as your right arm, and he isn't afraid or ashamed of boring you to death with them either. His gormless-looking wife, Izzie, makes matters far worse mollycoddling the cunt, cooing sympathy, and pandering to his stupidity.

Yes, Selena often said I was cold-hearted, and selfish, but I just can't stand being around weak-willed people, or anyone with illness, and I hate hospitals. I wouldn't visit her in the maternity unit after Bee was born. No chance.

That horrible invasive antiseptic smell, and all those sick people, puking and wailing, looking at me like it was my fault they're ill?

No. Not a cat in fucking hell's chance of that.

I've never moaned to anyone about my depression. I didn't bleat about all the time I spent in waiting rooms, to see some fucking quack who wanted to peddle pills, and recommend hours of counselling or therapy for me.

Nope. I gritted my teeth, bucked my ideas up, and got on with it. Yes, I'll admit I can be irritable, but in this day and age, who isn't? Selena said I had anger management problems too and, as Bee grew, she'd take sides with her,

'Mum's right, dad,' she'd say, 'You really ought to make an appointment to see the doctor.'

Well, that used to rile me more, make me angrier, but afterward, once the storm died down, I'd be swamped by remorse and guilt, feel so low, and utterly worthless.

I never meant to hurt them; never thought I'd raise a hand to anyone, let alone my own wife, or daughter.

Anyway, Bee left home. She married a local businessman when she was eighteen, and buggered off to Canada.

I don't hear from her much, except maybe a card now and then, you know? Birthdays or at Christmas when Selena was alive, but now she's gone, well, that's that.

I think they have a nipper. Jason, is it?

Something like that, anyway.

He's about the same age as the kid across the road.

That lad with the slope-headed dad, you know? The fair-haired young fella who's mum's down in my cellar. Speaking of which, I'd better go and switch on the monitor; find out what's she's up to. Oh, for fuck's sake, the stupid cow's pissed her pants. I just hope she hasn't shit as well, but now I'll have to go down there, clean her up. I'll have to listen to more mewling and whining, begging me to let her go as I give her a drink of water, or feed her. I don't know why I bother, to be honest. She won't need either the food or water soon anyway, and it really wouldn't hurt her to spend a few more hours sitting in her own mess, would it? *Who am I kidding?*

My conscience is bound to start nagging me, like it did whenever I lost my temper with Lena or Bee, and the guilt would build, like a weight on my shoulders, and I'd have to fuck off to the pub for a few bevvies.

Oh. Oh, wait, what's that?

I can see some action around number seventeen, and it looks as if lover-boy's home from wherever he's been. *Highway Maintenance* it says on the side of his van, but he must work away quite a lot. That's probably why the dog used to show off, and make so much noise. That was the final straw for me; one that broke the camel's back - a canine *Dawn Chorus*. Every morning at half-past seven; yap-yap-fucking-yap, a stupid shit-factory starts barking or howling, setting the other one going on Badger Close. Thirty minutes of constant din. Not any more though. I soon stopped that malarkey. Hey-ho, I gotta go. I ought to do it tonight really, you know? Get it over and done with, but I don't like the look of the wounds on her wrists, and I can't send her to the hereafter in a pair of shitty knickers, can I? Like a mug, I grab a First Aid box, and head to the cellar steps.

# Chapter Three

I tend not to pay much attention to the folk living on the Cres. I'm not really bothered about being neighbourly or wanting to know who's doing what or where. I mean, I know Postman Pat lives directly opposite, across the road in number thirteen, with his wife and kiddie. I think they both must have bounced on every branch of the ugly tree when they fell, but they're friendly enough. Always smile and wave, and I still get a card at Christmas.

I'm not sure who lives next to them in number fifteen because it's not long since been sold. In fact, the sign is still laid on the drive.

The Security bloke lives in number eleven, and then there's Jolly Hockey Sticks in number nine, with a weirdo of a husband. I call her Jolly Hockey Sticks because she reminds me of one of those posh St. Trinian-type girls, but without a straw boater, or sexy nylons. I could picture her wearing stockings, but definitely not the straw boater. What she sees in that gormless-looking husband of hers, I'll never know.

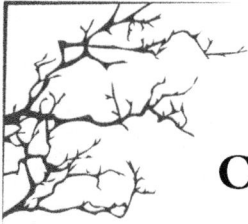

Obsessed with valeting the cars, he is. Weekend after weekend, he's out with a shammy and the polish, vacuum and duster. They have an Audi Quattro, and a Beamer, but never seem to go anywhere in them, other than work. I always say that Beamer drivers are wankers, and Audi has four zeroes on the front, and one behind the wheel. He's definitely a zero. She drives the Beamer, but I can't really call her a wanker, can I? Although, at times, I'll admit to conjuring up an image of her laid on a bed, in stockings; sliding a nimble finger down into the gusset of a pair of skimpy black silk panties. If I could watch her doing that, getting all hot and horny, I'd die a happy man, let me tell you. I'd actually like to hear her ask me to fuck her in that posh St Trinian's voice of hers too.

'Oh, please, Mister Mortimer, please slide your cock into me,' she'd whisper seductively, 'I'd love you to fuck me.'

Oh, yes. That would be tidy.

Mind you, Jolly Hockey Sticks is nowhere near as fit as Rearender Glenda, next-door-but-one to me, at number twenty. She lives with Bob the Builder now, so I have to pretend I don't know her when we pass on the Cres, even though we know each other intimately, I guess you could say. Jolly Hockey Sticks might be prissy-looking and a bit plain, but she's a damned site easier on the eyes than Misery Tits in twenty-six.

A black bloke lives in Jonathon's old place at twenty-eight, and Farty-Lil lives in number thirty.

When number seventeen went on the market, Misery Tits, Debbie, in twenty-six, said her cousin was thinking of buying it, until she found out the asking price. Lisa and Simon in number twenty-two were contemplating buying it for daughter, Amy, or at least lending her the deposit for it. Something like that. She did tell me one day, when I was in the queue at Lloyds Pharmacy on the main road, waiting for my prescription. She was behind me, wanting to buy something for Simon's athlete's foot. He works for the council as a bin man, and wearing safety boots all the time aggravates the condition.

That was the day I clattered the drug addict, if I remember rightly; a spotty-faced oik, with tattoos and piercings all over his face. For reasons unknown to me, smack-heads have their methadone doled out over the counter at pharmacists these days. It might be to stop them overdosing on it. I don't know. I don't care, and to be honest, I wish they'd all overdose. Anyway, this kid's rattling, desperate for an opiate fix, being abusive to staff about poor service and his need for what he insists is his right. He calls the young woman behind the counter a cunt, causing Lisa to gasp, and a flush of embarrassment to rise on the cheeks of the pharmacist. He gives her more grief, and gets really snotty when she asks him to calm down and take a seat. He ignores her request, and repeats his insult. That's when I add my two penn'orth,

'Look, kid, either watch your mouth or—'

'Or what, old man?' he interrupts.

I was going to say, 'or leave.'

'Come on, old timer,' he glares, 'or what?'

Through a red mist, I see metal glitter on his face - a nose ring, a lip piercing, and several loops in his ears - I can't stop myself, and don't really want to.

I rip the nose ring through the septum, tearing flesh, and druggie squeals as blood pours from the wound, but I ignore it. My other hand grabs metal in his ear, ripping and rending, to the sound of more gasps of surprise from Lisa. I cast the nose piercing aside, and hear it bouncing musically on the tiled floor as the lip loop is yanked free. I don't think about infected blood, HIV or anything else, other than smashing his balls with my knee, and flattening his arrogant nose with my fist.

The cops came, gave me a caution, but they couldn't do much else when the pharmacist and Lisa had told them what happened. They dragged the druggie away, pushed him into the back of a squad car and drove off.

I felt pretty good about the whole thing.

Anyhow, as things worked out, neither Misery Tits' cousin, nor Amy, moved into seventeen; it was her in the basement. Her and an ugly chimp of a husband, partner, or whatever it is they call them these days and, of course, the kiddie. I'm not sure if the kid's hers and his, or if it's from some previous relationship one of them had, but I reckon it's definitely ugly enough to be his.

They moved in about eighteen months ago, just as the bad winter started. I didn't like the look of them then.

He's a broad-shouldered, square-jawed, Neanderthal-looking bloke, with eyes too close together, and a bloody daft haircut. The young lad's had his cut the same way.

She's all Ugg boots, hair extensions, fake tan, and one of her fingernails is painted a different colour to the rest. Someone at the newsagents' shop said it was fashionable to have them like that. Fucking stupid is what I think it is.

About an hour after the removal van is empty, I see him upstairs in the front bedroom, with the light on, and no curtains over the window. He bends down, as bold as brass, and pulls off his joggers and shorts.

I'm completely gob-smacked.

I can see his pale, luminous hairy arse as plain as day, and he doesn't seem in the least bit concerned about his nakedness at all. In fact, he turns around, cock hanging on window sill, and the cheeky bastard waves at me. Yep. He smiles a big daft lopsided smile, and fucking waves at me. I jumped up, and drew my curtains quick-sharp, I can tell you. If Lena had been alive, she'd have been mortified. She'd have bent my ear about it for days, too. Of course, I'd have tuned it out, like I always did with her moaning. If I listened to her yapping it would drive me mad; make me want to slap her just to shut her up, but she'd have had fucking kittens if she'd been here when a caravan turned up the following morning. I wasn't best pleased about it either, but worse is yet to come. Oh, yes. The bare-faced, or bare-arsed, cheek of the chimp at number seventeen is yet to be fully revealed.

# Chapter Four

Well, that's put the tin hat on it now. I knew I should have just taken a polythene bag, a roll of insulating tape, and a knife down to the cellar with me, and done it. Put the bag over her head from behind, wind a couple of strips of tape around her neck at the bottom to seal it, and when she passes out, slit her throat; job done. Easy.

No. I have to feel sorry for her.

I have to let sympathy get the better of me.

Fuck-fuck-fuckety-fuck-fuck-fuck.

I snip the cable tie that holds her left wrist to the back of the chair, let her stretch it to get some of the circulation back, and then I bathe the wound and bind it with a gauze dressing and plaster. It looks quite nasty, to be honest.

She has pissed her pants, and shit them too, judging by the smell, and I suddenly think to myself, why on earth does she need clothes? She's not going anywhere but the hole in the back garden, and clothing is evidence.

I tell her to pull her arm out of the left sleeve of the grubby grey feather-print T-shirt and unhook her bra. The bra slips, and she tries putting her arm across her tits, but I pull it around to the back of the chair, and clamp it with another cable tie. I've seen tits before, and hers aren't any different; a couple of ripe oranges maybe, only not quite the same colour.

I repeat the process with the right arm. I ask her to slide it out of the T-shirt, which she does, and I take it off over her head. Then I relieve her of the bra, but she tries covering her tits again, so I slap her hand aside, grab it, and examine the groove cut into the wrist.

'Keep still, you stupid cow,' I tell her, 'I'm trying to help you.'

She mumbles something through the tape, and I can't tell what she's saying, so I ignore it.

I clean the wound, dress it, and then tie her arm to the back of the chair. I notice her knuckles are dark brown, or at least the wrinkled skin around them is, where fake tan has accumulated, but not rubbed in. I see that her elbows are the same. I don't really know why women bother with fake tan if they can't put it on properly.

'Right,' I say, looking her straight in the eyes, 'I'm going to release your ankles, clean your bits. Okay?'

She nods, but there's a weird look in her eyes.

'No funny business, though. Understand?'

Another nod, but slower this time, like she's mulling things over.

I cut the ties around her ankles, letting her stretch her legs, see her knees are as bad as her knuckles and elbows when it comes to fake tan stains.

The chafing on her ankles hasn't broken the skin, so I concentrate on getting her incontinence sorted out. I pull off her cream shorts, now yellowed at the crotch and wet through, with a few smudges of brown in the gusset.

'Jesus, lady, that stinks,' I say, gagging on the smell coming from soiled panties as I pull them from her hips, along her thighs, over her knees, and off her ankles.

Some of the crap smears on her skin, and she makes a kind of disgusted sound through the tape gag.

'Yeah, I know,' I agree, 'yucky, right?'

She nods and grunts.

I've filled a bucket with warm water, and a few drops of detergent liquid - the one that makes your hands feel as soft as your face, allegedly. It's the bucket I usually use to clean the car, and so is the sponge for that matter.

I soak the sponge; squeeze it, watching suds froth and drip, then begin to wash the crap from her calves, then her thighs, and finally, her lady's bits. She parts her thighs to let me clean her, but I can't really get to her arse, which is where the worst of the damage is.

'Stand up and face the wall,' I say to her, 'I'm going to clean your backside, but I don't want any showing off.'

She rises to her feet, sort of unsteadily, with her arms behind her back, tethered to the chair, and it must be quite tricky to manoeuvre. Eventually, I've enough space to wash the shit from her buttocks, and inside the cleft. She waits for me to finish wiping, and then slumps back onto the chair.

I can't tell if she's grateful or not, or feels any better about not sitting in her own mess anymore, but there's this look in her eyes as I bend to fasten her ankles back to the leg of the chair, you know? I never realised how vivid and blue her eyes are until now, and they're hypnotic to look into, even though they mirror the terror of imminent death.

Then her mouth is working against the tape, muffled words, incoherent, but almost intelligible too, echo from the walls of a damp cellar,

'Nnnurrr. Nnneerneee norrnoonoo. Nnneeeff.'

No. Let me talk to you. Please?

I start to shake my head, pull an ankle tight against a chair leg, ready to thread the tip of a cable tie into itself to secure it.

'Nnneeeff!' she mumbles, more agitated, yanking the leg free of my grip, 'Nnneerneee norrnoonoo!'

I think she's trying to escape at first, so I brandish a pair of scissors from the First Aid kit like a dagger,

'Calm down, missy. Just calm down,' I say to soothe her, but also intimidate her to silence, 'you're not going anywhere.'

Her shoulders sag, and she shakes her head,

'Nnnurrr. Noo noan nunnernaan.'

No. You don't understand?

'Understand what?' I ask.

'Nnneerneee norrnoonoo. Nnneeeff.'

'Okay,' I say, 'I'm going to remove the gag to give you a drink of water anyway, and when I do, you can say whatever it is you want to say, then you drink the water, and the gag goes back on, Got it?'

She nods, but I don't trust her.

'You scream, or make any moves I don't like,' I'm waving the tip of the scissors under her nose, 'and I'll stab you with these. Got it?'

Now, I know about Stockholm syndrome, because it was all over the news when Patty Hearst was kidnapped by the Symbionese Liberation Army - although who or what they were I had no idea. Stockholm syndrome is also used as the main theme for the film, *Dog Day Afternoon*, starring Al Pacino, where he takes the bank employees as hostages. The syndrome is an emotional attachment, a bond of interdependence between captive and captor that develops when someone threatens your life, deliberates, and doesn't kill you. I've never seen it in real life until I remove the tape over her mouth. She rubs a silky fake-tanned calf provocatively up the inside of my thigh, her eyes never leaving mine and, in a voice that has a strange accent which I'd never really noticed before, she says,

'Please don't kill me, Mister. If you let me go, I'll do anything you want.'

Her instep is teasing my cock, rubbing over the bulge of my bollocks, making it stir, as she adds,

'Anything. Honest. Just, please, let me go.'

Legs wrap around me, pulling me closer, thighs part wide; a vagina and neatly trimmed pubic hair are pushed into view as a lure; a honey trap. I pull back, slide around to the back of the chair, and tape her mouth shut,

'Fuck that, you filthy little cow,' I say, 'I wouldn't touch you with a ten-foot barge pole, lady, let alone stick my thingy in you. No fucking chance.'

# Chapter Five

I'm sitting on the edge of a sofa in the lounge, trying to relax, trying to get her out of my mind, trying to stop thinking about lithe, long legs wrapping around me, and the prospect of being able to do whatever I want with her. To blot it out, I put on a Melissa Etheridge disc, and think back to the day when things started to go horribly wrong.

They'd been bouncing the touring caravan around on the street for a couple of days, over the kerb, and onto a paved area in front of the house. She'd try to steer it as the hunky monkey supplied the brawn, but it was obvious to me that they hadn't got a clue what they were doing.

On and off it rolled, up and down, inching it closer to the bay window.

Why would you do that? I ask myself. Why would you block out the light? It must be pitch black in their lounge.

Then, one of those four-by-four things turns up, and a group of equally Neanderthal-looking blokes jump out of it, help manoeuvre the caravan into place.

This is apparently a cause for celebration at number seventeen, because within a couple of hours, several more Range Rovers, X5 Beamers, and a bloody huge fuck-off sized Navara truck thing are cluttering the Cres. They're double-parked, causing untold chaos for other residents, but they don't care. It's Miller time for ape-men.

I peer around the curtains at their antics; see a couple of chimps huddled at the kerbside behind the Navara. I wonder what kind of shenanigans they're up to, but don't find out until the morning after the party, when it pisses it down; a real torrential downpour.

Cases of beer are dragged from the boots of several badly-parked vehicles, taken through a side gate, into the kitchen at the back of the house.

Loud music reverberates against house fronts along the Cres; thudding bass booming as a rapper mumbles an indecipherable nursery rhyme over the top. That's all rap music is, you know? It's just sing-song nursery rhyme bollocks about niggers killing each other, fucking their bitches, and ho's, or whatever.

See, this is what really fucking riles me up. It's okay for them to call one another nigger, but if I did, coppers would be hammering on my door, calling me a racist, or saying I was inciting hate crime. Really? Have they ever once listened to the lyrics in those rap songs? Yes, I know they're indecipherable and incoherent crap, but check the lyrics of *Straight Up Nigga*, by Ice Tea, or *All Day*, by Kanye West. That's seriously demented shit there.

Just to set the record straight here, I wouldn't call the bloke living in Jonathon's old house a nigger. Yeah, he's black, but he's as English as tuppence, and anything but a nigger. He's a great bloke. I saw him in my local the other week, and he bought me a pint.

The party music is pumping at full volume now.

"Ride around listening to Sade, nigger. If you ain't with us, you in our way, nigger. You an actor, you should be on Broadway, nigger, cause you do shit the broad way, nigger. Your bitch got an ass, but my broad way thicker."

This racist, misogynistic bullshit is being piped out to the residents of the Cres, at high volume, until half-past three in the morning, accompanied by a choir of tone-deaf voices from a dozen drunken knuckle-draggers.

I'm unemployed, so I don't have to be up and about early in the morning, but Postman Pat does, Jolly Hockey Sticks' weird car-cleaning-obsessed hubby does. Misery Tits Debbie's husband, John, is an early riser as well, so someone calls the cops. Someone has the decency and the bollocks to make an anonymous tip-off about the noise nuisance from number seventeen.

It wasn't me, as Shaggy insisted, but, if you'll pardon the horrible term, I'm being fingered for the dirty deed. I am the one whose house is pointed at, talked about by the drunken thugs congregating around the caravan. I don't actually see this happen. I've decided to get some shut-eye in the back bedroom. It used to be Bee's and, because I never had the heart or energy to be bothered redecorating, it has a kind of teenage theme to it, you know? Britney Spears and Justin Timberlake posters on one wall, Avril Lavigne and Christina Aguilera opposite, and boxes of CD's stashed under the bed.

I should have a clear out, buy a few rolls of wallpaper and a couple of tins of emulsion, but I don't want to erase the fact that I had a daughter. I know I wasn't the best dad in the world, and I could've shown her more love and affection, less anger and irritation but, what is, is. I can't change it now. She's in Canada with her hubby and Jason. I'm sure it's Jason. I'm here with memories, and a tribe of misfits living opposite; the new neighbours from Hell.

I wake up the following morning, and hear John, out in the garden. I don't know what he's doing, but the shed door is ajar, and it sounds like a saw is being revved up to cut timber. Misery Tits Debbie is always nagging the poor bastard to do some job or other around the house. She's worse than Lena. Always on the soft fucker's case about something that needs doing, and I tell you, if I was John, well, she'd be sporting a fat lip, and a shiner on a regular basis. *Bitch.*

Yes, I know it makes me sound no better than those misogynistic niggers I was ranting about, but she really would try the patience of a saint. I hear her Harpy scream from inside the house, yelling his name, summoning her personal slave for more chores, more toil, and more tasks.

I pour this month's contents of my mail shredder into a polythene bag, glance out of a window to see black rain clouds gathering on the horizon, not knowing about the shit-storm that will erupt very soon.

I haul the bag to an incinerator at the bottom of the garden, pour strips of accumulated junk mail into it, and then strike a match. Wind whips up to snuff the flame and I curse,

'Fuck!'

John hears me during a lull in his timber cutting, and saunters to the gap in the fence. We've both talked about repairing the faulty panel but, to be honest, we still like to have our secret tête-à-tête meetings here to chew the cud, swap gossip, or just gripe about women. I used to moan about Lena, and he dished up dirt on Debbie. He's the one who came up with her nickname of Misery Tits.

'Burning the bumf, Stan?' he says, catching me off guard as I scrutinise a tiny flame flickering at the base of the incinerator, hoping it will survive the stiff breeze. He calls it bumf, but I always used to joke with Lena about my weekly cremation of accumulated flyers. I called it the Bonfire of Inanities, which she realised, because she was well-read and almost as intelligent as me, was a play on the title of the 1987 Tom Wolfe novel, *The Bonfire of the Vanities*. Over time, the novelty of the pun wore off, but the name stuck. I'd be wasting my time explaining it to John, so I laugh,

'Yeah, cremating crap again.'

Since I turned fifty, the shit they send out to me has increased exponentially, and I get two or three per day. I feel sorry for people like Postman Pat opposite, who have to lug sack loads of this bollocks around to deliver it to people who don't give a flying fuck about it. There must be millions of *Aviva*, or *Legal and General* letters posted each week, begging people to part with hard-earned cash, and take out life insurance with them. Some of them use over-the-hill celebrities, like Michael Parkinson, in their advertisements. Well, I reckon he can afford to shell out the premiums for shit like that, but I'm out of work, and I can't, so fuck him, and his free pen. He gets shredded and burned like all the rest.

'They were making a right racket last night, weren't they?' he hooks a thumb in the direction of the Cres, and I know who he means.

'Oh, the caravan crew at seventeen?'

'Yeah,' he giggles, 'Debbie called the coppers out at half-past three, asked them to send a patrol car, and tell them to keep their noise down. Not that it did any good, mind.'

'I was in the back bedroom, so I never heard a peep.'

'You were lucky, mate. Once the rap music stopped, it was football chants, and rugby songs for over an hour.'

I stand back, admiring the blaze, grinning as Michael Parkinson's face blackens and curls, or at least a shredded jigsaw picture of him does.

'Where are they from?' I ask, not really caring, but at least trying to make conversation.

'Manchester, I think,' John says, 'but they might be travellers, you know? Irish tinkers. They sounded Irish.'

'They sounded like ignorant twats to me, John.'

A cloud scuds across the horizon as an anxious frown flits over John's face,

'Have you, ah, have you, ah, you know, like, checked your car this morning, Stan?'

There's a hollow sensation in the pit of my stomach as I say,

'No. Why?'

'Oh, just wondered, only we saw a couple of them, last night, scuttling back across the road, giggling, about half-an-hour after the feds turned up.'

The hollow pit is filled by a ball of dread.

John knows there's something wrong with my car, I can tell. He knows those bastards have been up to no good with it, as sure as eggs are eggs.

'Okay, thanks,' I say, 'I'll check it now.'

I'm a couple of yards from our illicit meeting place on my way to my back door, when I hear a voice echoing after me down the garden path,

'Sorry, Stan. I thought you'd seen it, mate.'

Fuck-fuck-fuck! What have the bastards done to it?

My bottom jaw is flapping as the first droplets of rain spatter the rear windshield of my silver Seat Ibiza, and I see the wiper is missing; broken off at the motor pivot. It annoys me, sure, but not quite as much as the one word of personal abuse daubed in cream emulsion across the boot in foot-high letters; *Cunt.*

*Rhythm is a Dancer*, but anger is a cancer. It's a big fat malignant tumour that grows and festers inside you. I first noticed mine as a teenager, felt the adrenalin buzz of losing my temper with another kid who was pestering me during geography class. He'd forgotten his pen, wanted me to lend him one, hissing in my ear,

'Stan. Stan, lend us a pen will you, mate?'

I ignored him as best I could, concentrating instead on a lurid coloured contour map of Africa, copying it into my exercise book, but he kept it up,

'Come on, Morty,' he whined, 'lend me one.'

I shook my head, hunched over the desk, but then he pushed me one step too far. He started to kick the back of my chair in an incessant rhythm, occasionally letting a toe slip through the gap to prod my buttocks.

'Go on, Stan, give me a pen.'

I'd had enough. I gripped my Platignum like a dagger, twisted in my seat and plunged it through his cheek, impaling a flapping tongue with a nib in a shower of blood and blue-black ink.

Eyes bulged in shock, and a striped snake slithered from the corner of his mouth, down his chin, onto a crisp white shirt.

My anger cancer metastasised from that point onward to dominate my life; to infiltrate or spoil relationships, but at the same time, make me euphoric.

I've become an adrenalin addict. I revel in the shakes and quakes of volcanic rage, as my internal magma chamber grows closer to spewing out its searing fury, deluging the unsuspecting.

Cunt?

Well, Danish King I may be. A Berk, I most certainly am, because Lena and Bee told me often enough, one way or the other, but, when a bunch of shit-for-brains paint it on the boot of my car, I'm not inclined to take that lying down, see? I can't prove it was them, but I know it was.

I'll show them who's a cunt.

That's when I decide to install my CCTV system, and get my own back, of course, but the rain brings an added bonus; one that stirs things up good and proper.

# Chapter Six

I'm absolutely soaked to the fucking bone when I've finished scraping the back end of the car. It's a good job they didn't use gloss, or Hammerite, otherwise I'd have to drive around in a Cuntmobile forever.

I head indoors, strip out of sticky wet jeans and T-shirt in the lounge, pulling off my underwear and socks on the stairs - a bit like when I was having the affair with Glenda from work - and dive into a welcome hot shower.

As I'm soaping my bits, I think of Rearender Glenda, and how close we came to wrecking our relationships, but the sex? Oh, boy, now that was sex. Thinking about it as I'm in the shower makes me rock hard, and I slide a soapy hand up and down a slippery shaft, occasionally stroking my balls, or pointing needle-like jets of the shower head at my groin to let hot water help me along toward ecstasy.

I don't have sex these days, at least not with anyone else in the room. It's Madame Palm, and five daughters if I do, and my reflection in the wardrobe mirror, not that I like to watch myself jerking off, but hey-ho. Needs must.

I shoot a thick creamy rope of jizz at tiles; shudder as I imagine Glenda's mouth sucking me, grab a warm towel from the rail, and wrap it around my dripping torso.

I walk into the front bedroom, rummage in a chest of drawers for clean socks and underwear, spray deodorant under my pits, and splash a bit of aftershave on my chops. I'm headed back to the bathroom when I glance out of the bay window.

Fuck!

It's coming down in stair rods outside, gutters full to the brim with dirty brown water, rolling and bubbling like a witch's cauldron, from the top of the Cres to the bottom.

Outside number seventeen, however, the Rashid is being diverted to join the Dumyat. Okay, I'm sorry about that. Maybe you won't quite understand my analogy, using the rivers of the Nile Delta, but essentially, the water flowing down the gutter on the odd-numbered, shorter curve of the Cres, is crossing the road to join the flood water in gutters on the even-numbered, longer curve of the Cres.

The gutter outside number seventeen is blocked by a recently-installed tarmac ramp and, when I say recently, I mean last fucking night, either before or after my car was vandalised, but probably before. I remember the scrum at the kerbside behind the Navara, and I suspect that was what they were doing. I can't prove it, but I'm pretty sure it was them. It definitely wasn't there yesterday, and my carefully-tended garden was. Now the ramp is there, but the flowerbed at the bottom of my front lawn, tiny as it was, is being washed away by a deluge of water from the hastily-erected dam.

Plants and shrubs I spent weeks cultivating, nurturing and tending in a greenhouse, are gone, blocking drains, and creating a monumental lake.

I'm incandescent, effulgent in a red-misted rage, as fists clench and unclench in synchronous spasms to match those of muscles in my jawline. I cannot utter even the most basic of curses or expletives to express my loss. It is almost as bad as the day Doctor Fucking Smarmy told me that Lena's pancreatic cancer was not only inoperable, but liable to kill her very shortly too.

The cherry on the cake is Neanderthal man, dragging his knuckles to the front of his cave, dressed in a high-viz waterproof overcoat, puffing on a cigarette, oblivious to the carnage he has created; the defilement of Lena's final resting place and memorial garden. *Bastard!* He wouldn't be able to read, or pronounce, any of the names of plants swamped and washed away, or any of the Latin ones for that matter. He should be the one driving around with the word *Cunt* emblazoned on the rear of his diesel-guzzling four-by-four shit wagon.

What is it, anyway?

A Mitsubishi fucking Pajero?

Crap.

Then I have an idea. Well, it's more of an epiphany, despite living on the Cres, and not the road to Damascus.

I'll show you, you imbecile.

I fire up the computer.

# Chapter Seven

With only a towel wrapped tightly around me, I sit at a desk in a reclining black leather chair, perusing the local council's website looking for the key to his demise.

I open a tab for *Highway Maintenance*, which I think is pretty ironic, considering that this is emblazoned along the side of a works' van, parked behind the caravan.

I scan a list of options;

Highway Closures? Highway Development?

Nope.

Road Improvement Request? Road works?

No. That's not it. Ah, here we are,

Roads and Pavements - Report a problem.

I work my way through the usual minefield of jargon, civil servant gibberish or claptrap, eventually finding the part where I report a problem directly, either by phone, by letter, or via email. *Who writes fucking letters anymore?*

I decide email the best option for several reasons.

The first is that if I could be arsed to write a letter to the council, my fingerprints would be all over the paper and envelope, my DNA on the envelope and stamp in the form of saliva samples, and they'd have a sample of my handwriting too. Call me paranoiac or call me a cab, but I don't trust authority of any kind, so fuck you very much.

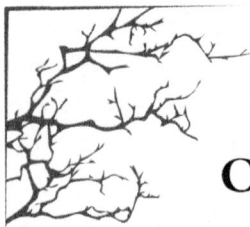

I could make a telephone call, but then they'd have my number, which I don't want them to have, and worse, I'd have to speak to a jumped-up girlie, with the attention span of a tadpole, and the intelligence quotient of a gnat. We'd spiral into ever-decreasing circles and, as happened at parents' evening, when Bee was fourteen, my anger is bound to overspill, and things become unpleasant. I don't like to lay blame at anyone's door, but Miss Forster was, and probably still is, a miserable pedantic cunt.

I've been around a bit, and know stuff; general sort of knowledge stuff. It sticks in my head, rattles through the cranium into filing systems I don't understand, or need to. It's there. It stays there until I need it or need to pass it on. Bee asks me what *sushi* is. I tell her that it's the way the Japanese serve raw fish; usually with vinegar-soaked rice.

'Miss Forster says *sushi* is raw fish, dad. She told us that the Japanese word for raw fish was *sushi*.'

'And?' I ask, but needn't have, because I know what she's going to tell me.

'I told her that she was wrong, and that *sashimi* is the word for raw fish.'

'So, what did she do then, sweet-pea?'

'She accused me of being truculent, and gave me an hour's detention. It's unfair. I was right, wasn't I, dad?'

'Yes, you were right, and she was wrong, but I'll tell you what we're going to do.'

'What?'

'When's the next parents' evening?'

'End of term, in two weeks, why?'

'Well, you do the detention, Bee, like a good girl, and you leave Miss Forster to me, okay?'

She's a bit sullen about it, as any teenager would be, because she usually has plans for her Friday evenings, so having an hour stripped from her time doesn't go down too well.

'All right,' she reluctantly agrees, 'but promise me you'll sort it out.'

'Oh, I will.'

'What does truculent mean, anyway?'

'Quick to argue or fight, sweet-pea, but your old man will show high and mighty Miss Forster what truculence really looks like when I see her.'

Lena casts me a warning glance, but I shrug it off.

When I'm seated opposite the prim and prissy missy, my hackles are rising, and Lena is patting my hand in her usual 'keep calm, Stan' manner, but it's too late for that.

'Tell me, Miss Forster,' I say, all sweetness and light, 'I was under the impression that this was a school.'

'It is,' she says.

'Really?' I goad, 'A place for education, if I'm not mistaken - *in loco parentis* - which is Latin for *in place of the parent*, if I remember rightly.'

'Yes, that's right, but—'

I raise a hand to silence her *but*, wanting to kick her butt, as the Americans say in all the good films.

'*Educo*, also Latin, meaning, *I lead, I train*, yes?'

'Yes, but—'

'So, when I trained or lead my daughter to believe a thing to be true, educated her in, say for instance, nuances or the mis-interpretations of a language, then why would a person, elected by this establishment to assist education, not only undermine what I have taught her in the past, but punish her for said knowledge?'

'I don't understand, Mister Mortimer. I have never—'

I rise to my feet, as my voice rises above the general hubbub of insignificant conversation, in a hall packed to the rafters with other staff, and parents, to state,

'Exactly, Miss Forster! Non intellegetis! Anata wa rikai shite inai!'

'What? Why are you shouting Mister Mortimer?'

'I'm shouting because you are plainly stupid, Miss Forster; a fucking dullard! You don't understand in Latin, and you don't understand in Japanese. So, I'm trying to hammer through the thick, arrogant fucking skull of yours that the Japanese for raw fish is fucking *sashimi*, and not bastard *sushi*!'

Lena is making shushing sounds at my left, in time to gasps of astonishment from onlookers to my right.

Miss Hoity-toity Forster rises, red-faced,

'I think you'd better leave Mist—'

'I think you'd better shut the fuck up, you halfwit, and the next time you call my daughter *truculent*, or give her a detention for trying to teach you something, educate you, or enlighten you in a linguistic error, I suggest you think otherwise, you vile bitch!'

She slaps me then.

She actually slaps my face.

Well, guess what Stan "the man" Mortimer did?

He slapped her back, good and hard. *Bitch.*

I didn't literally slap her back, obviously.

I slapped her face in retaliation, and stormed off.

Lena was hot on my heels, jabbering about me going over the top, about blowing things out of proportion, and making a fuss and hoo-ha in front of all the other parents.

I told her straight; I didn't give a flying fanny about the rest of the parents, or what those shit-for-brains might think. All I cared about was Bee, see?

She wouldn't let it go; hounding me until we arrive home, and have an almighty ding-dong battle, face to face and toe to toe, squaring up. That's when I bit her cheek. I don't know why, maybe it was from watching *Silence of the Lambs* that prompted it, or maybe just plain old anger, but, hey-ho. I hold my hand up. I'm not proud of what I did, but a done bun can't be undone, right?

There was a hastily arranged meeting of minds in the headmaster's office; all the usual razzamatazz, but in the end, they did fuck-all about it. They daren't. I had the cunt bang to rights. Well, now I've got a knuckle-dragger bang to rights about unapproved, unlawful modifications to the pavement and highway at the foot of his property.

I've selected email to report his misdemeanour, but I am not stupid enough to let them have my real name, real email address, or postcode for that matter.

I'm minus a rear windscreen wiper, and was almost the proud driver of a Cuntmobile, so I want to make sure that, other than my IP address, they get squat diddley.

I should have sent it from the library really, and then the IP address for my computer would remain secret too, but I wasn't thinking too clearly.

Lena's resting place is washed away, my front garden looks like monsoon season in Bangla-fucking-desh, and I'm watching an overgrown inbred smoke another fag at the kerb edge watching it all happen.

I create a fictitious email address, using a name I've cobbled together using an anagram form of a well-known heavy metal band. Metallica became Alice Malt, residing at number 46 Badger Close, telephone number withheld.

I fill out the online form for the council, telling them about the modification to the pavement and kerb, stating that planning permission must be obtained for vehicular crossing, and using approved contractors to undertake the work to complete this. I add how shocked I am, hope that the matter will be resolved as soon as possible, and I click on the *Send* icon. *No, it isn't a button, it's an icon, but not one a simian smoker would cherish, worship or revere.*

I waited and watched.

Days drag out, protracted to become almost a week, before, one morning, a van comes to a sedate halt outside number seventeen with a squeal of brakes. A rather heated discussion takes place between a man from the council, armed with a shovel, and Mighty Joe Young, but in the end, there's a smile on my lips.

The tarmac is flung into the back of the vehicle with a wagging finger of admonishment and, I'm so happy, I retire to the bathroom, take a hot shower, and wonderful wank, thinking very hard about Jolly Hockey Sticks, in a pair of sheer black nylons, with the seam up the rear, and maybe my semen up her rear too.

My triumph, much like my masturbation session, is to be short-lived, and definitely not end as pleasantly.

# Chapter Eight

I was born in sixty-six, which was the year England last won the World Cup, and I used to spend my days as a kid, watching loads of television. It was mostly crap when I think back on it. *Fireball XL5*, *Stingray* and *Supercar*, but dad's favourite was *The Beverley Hillbillies*, which was an American sitcom featuring the Clampetts; a bunch of hick country folk, who find oil on their land, become rich, and move to California.

When the new family moved in at number seventeen, they reminded me so much of the Clampetts that I started to mentally refer to them that way. The simian husband is Jethro Bodine, and the woman in my cellar is Elly May.

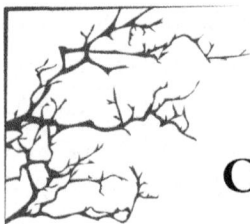

I put Melissa Etheridge back in her case, turn off the hi-fi, and make some supper. It's nothing fancy, but I can cook, have quite a wide repertoire, and actually enjoy the preparation process too, you know? Slicing onions and so forth is relaxing, soothing almost. I throw a Chilli Con Carne together, leave it to simmer on low heat, chugging a couple of cheap lagers along the way, and take a squint at what Elly May is up to in the cellar. It looks as though she's nodding off on the chair, chin on her chest, lolling to one side. *That can't be comfortable, and she'll end up with a crick in her neck if I leave her.* Now, I don't know if this is part of the Stockholm syndrome, and if I'm being exploited by it, or exploring it myself, but I decide that I can't just leave her like that. She may be my prisoner, and yes, when I reach the point of no return, I'm going to kill her to keep her quiet. I have to. We both know it. *So, why not make what little time she has left at least comfortable, and let her have some fucking dignity in death?*

I may not be in the best of shape, but I reason I'm fit enough to drag a mattress from the single bed in the back bedroom down a couple of flights of stairs into the cellar. I'll let her sleep on that. I still have a pair of handcuffs in the back of a wardrobe from when me and Glenda used to play bondage games on our afternoons off. I can use those to fasten her to the main gas pipe, no problem. I reckon I've enough control over her to make her see that if she shows off and makes a scene, well, she knows what will happen. I shrug to the monitor and climb the stairs.

I've worked up quite a sweat by the time I disturb her slumber, letting the mattress flop onto the stone floor with a slap, and she looks up at me, all bleary-eyed, but with a kind of grateful gleam in there too.

'Okay,' I say, 'I'm going to snip these cable ties, put some cuffs on you, and tether you to this pipe over here, see?'

She nods and makes a sound through the tape gag. I think it sounded like 'Thank you,' although I wouldn't swear to it. She might have said 'Fuck you,' but I doubt it.

'Once you're secure, I'll fetch you some supper, and then we can have a little chat. I have a few questions that are bugging me, and I'd like some answers. Deal?'

Another nod and genuine gratitude in her eyes.

The cable ties fall to the floor, and she stretches stiff limbs, rubbing points of restraint, and aching muscles. As the tape gag is peeled noisily from her mouth, she wets her lips, smiles and whispers,

'Thank you.'

'Don't mention it,' trots off my tongue before I can stop it, and I know it sounded stupid, but it's too late.

One bracelet of the cuffs snaps around her wrist, and I have a flashback to the first time I used them on Glenda.

We're at her place, and her hubby is working away, at some conference or other in Birmingham, or maybe it was Brighton. I didn't care. All I knew was that I had the whole day to have fun with her. Working at John Lewis meant we had a full day off each week, and we selected it so that it coincided with one another's, and the days when Lena would be at work too. Glenda had been reading about bondage on the net, wanted to try it, wanted to surrender her body, be forced to do stuff that she normally would anyway, but pretend it was against her will, if that makes sense?

She had this big brass headstand on her double bed, so I looped the cuffs through it, and snapped them around her wrists. She had such thin wrists and small hands that I thought she could probably slip out of them, but I knew she wouldn't want to. It would spoil the illusion for her. She stretched out, arms above her head, purring like a cat on heat, rubbing one stocking-clad leg over the other, in a rustle of silky seduction. Her green eyes flashed lust from under a bob cut of blonde hair, and my cock was straining at the leash. I was as hard as iron that first time.

Nervous fingers fumbled with studs on a suspender belt, careful not to ladder the nylons as I unhooked them. I knew what she'd paid for them, and they weren't cheap, so if I didn't damage them she could wear them again. I rolled them down her milky thighs one by one, letting the slack drop over each knee, sliding to her ankles, gossamer thin. She's moaning in the back of her throat, letting the animal instinct take over as her passion builds, ready to do my bidding, no matter what.

My throat was dry as I licked my lips in anticipation. I could hardly contain my arousal, tenting my underwear, pushing a throbbing member to the front of my trousers. The panties were eased off as slowly as the stockings, and her ripe moistness slick, glinting in sunlight.

'So, what's bothering you, mister?' snaps me back to the here and now, with Elly May.

She's coiled on a mattress, legs tucked under her, but no longer trying to protect her modesty, or hide any of her body from my gaze; vulnerable, almost wanton.

'Let me fetch supper first, and then we'll talk.'

'Okay.'

'No fucking tricks mind, missy. I can easily eat your supper after I've put you in the ground, you know?'

'I know,' she husks warily, 'I'll be good.'

'Promise?' I ask, like a teenager who's been told he could put his tongue into a girl's mouth for the first time, or maybe feel inside her knickers in the playground.

'Promise,' she says.

Stockholm syndrome?

I return with two bowls of chilli and two spoons, a plate of grated cheese, a few Nachos, and a large bowl of steaming rice.

I sit on the chair as she folds her long legs under her buttocks at the edge of the mattress. She spoons a portion of rice into her chilli bowl, adds cheese, and nibbles the corner from a Nacho.

'This is good,' she says, 'Did you make it?'

'Yeah,' I reply, 'thanks. Glad you like it.'

'So what did you want to know?'

From my own experience of psychoanalysis, I know that what happens next is transference. I see Elly May as a different person now for several reasons, each important, but undermining my determination. We've broken bread together, so to speak, by having a late night supper in her cell. She's wearing cuffs from an intense sexual situation I experienced with someone I found irresistible. Lastly, she's opening up to me, exhibiting signs that she is less threatened, despite the fact that she knows I'm going to kill her. I'm mulling this over whilst she waits for my answer, but then she throws me a curve ball,

'What time is it, Mister?'

# Chapter Nine

For a week after the tarmac ramp incident, there's a lull in the activities at seventeen, until the Pajero's alarm wrenches me from my slumbers at 4:30 in the morning. I throw the duvet aside, stomp to the bay window, and peer around the side of a curtain. I'm as naked as the day I was born but, unlike Jethro, I'm not happy to be seen with my cock on a windowsill, so the curtain is kept in place to preserve my modesty.

Indicators flash rhythmically, in time to the honking horn, *barp-barp-barp-barp*-fucking-*barp*, over and over, and I'm waiting for someone in the house to point a fob at the damned thing, press a button, and stop the noise.

No. That doesn't happen, and I have to conclude that, either they sleep the sleep of the damned, in some kind of comatose state where they're immune to the din, or that they're not in the house.

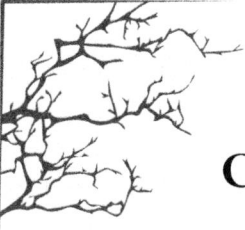

It must be on some sort of timer, because after maybe five minutes, it stops. Either that or my willpower is a lot stronger than I gave it credit for, and I'm telekinetic. No, of course I'm not telekinetic. If I were, once the nuisance noise started up again after ten minutes of golden silence, I would have been able not only to end the fucking racket, but also levitate the Pajero to hurl it several miles across the face of the planet, or through their lounge window. I can make out a mobile telephone number on a transparent strip in the rear windshield. Underneath is a partial sign, it says, *Gardening Services*, or it used to, but now it simply reads *arden vices.* I jot down the number, dress hastily, and pull on my shoes to head out to a BT payphone kiosk at the junction of Badger Close and Stag Lane. They're not getting my home number or my mobile. I know it's going to cost me, but, so what? I'll keep it short and to the point.

I insert my 60p, putting a fistful of spare change on a small shelf by the phone, and dial the number. It's picked up on the fifth ring,

'Who the fuck is this?' an irate voice demands.

'The alarm on your Pajero is keeping me awake.'

'It's ten-past five in the bastard morning, you cunt.'

'Exactly, so sort it out, cunt.'

'It's not mine, I sold it last week.'

The line goes dead before I can insert any more cash.

Not bad for a quid, but I'm no wiser as to how to stop the alarm. I settle for sleeping in the back bedroom. The trouble is, during the day, when Jethro's out and about maintaining highways, the Pajero is still making a God-awful racket.

Misery Tits Debs calls the cops again, but they're not interested. They suggest banging on the door of the house or phoning the owner. She gets the same abuse I did.

Eventually, Jethro returns, lifts the bonnet, scratches his head and his bollocks alternately, makes a couple of calls standing at the kerb smoking, occasionally stabbing the air with the hot end of the fag as punctuation.

After ten minutes, Jethro is joined by one of his party animals, and together they peer under the bonnet, probing and pointing, tugging cables, generally dickering around, but solving nothing. Jethro jumps in, starts it up to take it for a spin, and returns at around six o'clock, with Elly by his side in the front seat of the Pajero. They have armfuls of pizza boxes, a couple of big bottles of soda, and the kid with the shit haircut. The kid's brought a mate with him.

They all scamper off into the house, but the jeep isn't finished being a nuisance. Jethro is obviously as annoyed by it as residents of the Cres, but try as he might, he can't stop the alarm from sounding every quarter of an hour.

An RAC van appears at around seven-thirty, and the patrolman, recovery man, or whatever they're called, rolls up his sleeves and sets to work. The noise is less frequent, but the RAC man shakes his head, climbs into his bright orange van, and buggers off - probably for a pizza. Elly has been mincing around the arse-end of jeep for the last quarter-of-an-hour, sliding slippery slices of stuffed crust salami-coated shite into her greedy maw as though it was going out of fashion.

I hate fast food. I can't abide it, won't eat it, and object to the fucking smell of it, but they seem to thrive on it.

In between regular disturbances by the jeep's alarm, there is an endless parade of delivery vehicles; driven by swarthy-looking Asians mostly, but all clutching parcels of hot greasy crap, from various nations, under their arms. It gives me an idea, well, truth be told, it actually prompts two ideas; one of which is a way to disturb their peace and quiet on a regular basis, the other is more drastic. It's a way to get rid of the noisy fucking jeep once and for all.

It really is amazing what you can learn from a bit of research on the internet.

# Chapter Ten

Elly answered most of my questions, but in her own way, and I had the impression she was holding something back from me most of the time. I asked why her husband, boyfriend or partner wasn't agitated or alarmed by her absence, why he hadn't called the cops to report her missing. I know it's a myth that you have to wait twenty-four hours to file a report.

She was shifty about things, sketchy with detail, and I seemed to be wrestling eels whilst wearing rubber gloves. Then, she pushes the Stockholm buttons again, sliding her long limber fake-tanned leg up mine, to my crotch, as I'm perched on the edge of the chair.

'I really ought to thank you for supper,' she husks.

I remove the foot resting at my groin firmly, if a little reluctantly,

'No, it's fine, as long as you enjoyed it.'

'Look,' she says, 'I know I'm going to die, one way or another, but I hope when you kill me you do it quickly, and without pain.'

I'm uncomfortable talking about how I'll end her life, and want to change the subject, but that's awkward.

I either continue asking questions which she has no intention of answering, let her use her seductive charms to divert me from being honest about her imminent death, or I tell her exactly how, and when, it will happen.

That's the bind.

I don't want to murder her, unless I have to, unless I reach the point of no return, see? So, I can't tell her when that's liable to be, and also, I don't want to go into too much gory detail about how I'll do it. To be honest, my plans keep changing like my moods. I don't want it to be a long, painful thing, but at the same time, I'd like it not to be messy either. I'll have to clean up afterwards. I tend to think that quick is usually messy; the two go hand-in-hand, not that I've had much previous experience. This is my first time. *It's hers too, you soft twat.*

'What's your name?' I ask.

It's the first non-death-related question that pops into my head, but by this point in our interactions, no matter what her real name is, she's always going to be Elly May to me. She tells me, and I file it away, but promise myself I'll try to use it when I have to, out of respect.

'What's yours?' she asks in a quid pro quo tone.

'Stan,' I reply, almost adding, 'the man, Mortimer.'

No real point in keeping my name secret.

She reclines onto her elbows, a chain rattling pipe as the cuffs prevent her moving too far, stretches out those enticing long, lithe legs, lifts an arrogant chin to gaze at me with piercing blue eyes.

'Whatever you decide, Stan, I will forgive you. You are a kind man.'

No, I'm not. I'm not kind at all.

My mind is in turmoil now, because Lena said more or less the same thing when she found out about me and Glenda. She blamed herself for it, said I was a kind man, led astray by my emotions, and my desires.

You see, when we first hooked up, Lena and I had a healthy sex life, very healthy indeed. I mean, the Duracell Bunnies would have had trouble keeping up with us, and it was on a regular basis too. We couldn't keep our hands off each other, couldn't get enough of one another. I was stable and happy; happier than I've ever been, and I was over the moon when she fell pregnant with Bee.

Then post-partum depression kicked in, and the rift began, gradually inching wider to become a chasm, until, in the end, it was an abyss. Neither of us saw it coming, and neither of us did anything about it.

I wasn't a kind man. I was an insensitive shit; selfish, motivated by masculinity, and my cock. She forgave me my sins though, as I forgave her for having me sectioned under the Mental Health Act after the fiasco at the school. Those were dark times. She'd probably have me sectioned again if she saw what I'm up to with the Clampetts. Elly's smiling serenely at me, watching emotions playing across my face, trying to interpret them, trying to gauge what I'm thinking as her left foot deftly massages my groin. There's no need for words. *Stockholm syndrome?* I utter them anyway,

'I'd better go,' I mumble in a dry throat.

'Stay,' she begs, 'please.'

'I can't. It wouldn't be right.'

Left foot remains on my penis, as a right knee rolls out, parting thighs, exposing a neatly-trimmed triangle of black pubic hair, and nestling within, moist labia.

'Please, Stan, stay. I will make it right.'

Like a zombie, I rise from the chair, let it topple over backward onto the cold stone floor. As I unbutton a shirt, she watches me tug tails from the waistband of trousers, and let her try to convince me that she can indeed make it right.

# Chapter Eleven

I'm sitting at my computer, giggling like a schoolgirl menaced by a flasher, mobile phone clutched in one hand as fingers of my other hover over the keyboard.

I purchased one of those cheap pay-as-you-go SIMs, registered to Alice Malt's email address, but I also started using the same bogus address to register for loads of other shit too; free shit. In this day and age, everyone seems to want to give stuff away, and all they want in return are a few simple details like name, address, telephone number and, of course, a valid email account. *A confirmation link has been sent to AliceMalt@yahoo.co.uk. Please use this to verify your email account.* It's as easy as taking a bag of sweeties from a kid, to be honest.

Name: Jethro Bodine

Address: 17 Longridge Crescent.

Windows automatically saves all the information for me, including pesky fucking passwords that you have to try to remember or write down, so on most sites, I let the *Autofill* function do its job.

Catalogues, quotations for all manner of useless stuff; applications for credit and debit cards too, so the postman will be littering the doormat of the Clampetts on a daily basis. I just hope it isn't the poor sap that lives at number thirteen having to lug it to their door.

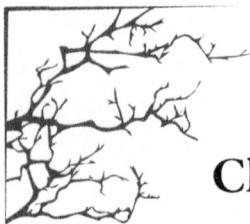

I'm not finished there though. Oh, no. Not by a long fucking chalk, because I'm printing off a list of takeaway emporia in the neighbourhood, with phone numbers.

If the Clampetts like their junk food so much, well, I'll make sure they have a steady supply, from a selection of menus. Some places charge for delivery, but I don't give a rat's arse about that, and don't care if the food is wasted after they try to deliver it, because as I said before, all of it is absolute garbage.

The best part is going to be fucking-up that stinking diesel heap of shite with the faulty alarm; the Pajero, and, thanks to the Worldwide Web, I know just how to do it.

During my days of counselling and therapy, I learned a lot about psychological conditioning and so forth; how a mind works, how it could be programmed, or in my case re-programmed, to think in different ways. Over the past seven days, the residents of the Cres have grown used to the erratic behaviour of the alarm on Jethro's jeep, kind of conditioned to accept it. They take no notice of it now, and, to be honest, I can sleep through it too, but choose not to. I monitor the times when the damned thing kicks off, make a note of it, and gradually see a pattern emerge.

Okay, during the daytime, the jeep isn't always there, because a highway maintenance van is parked in its place on the drive, next to the caravan, but, when it's there, I've discovered it usually goes off at around lunchtime. I don't know why, but it does. Jethro is out, Elly is out, and the kid with the daft haircut is at school, or with friends of the Clampetts, but the alarm goes off.

It also goes off at 4:30 in the morning without fail, and at eleven o'clock at night. Those two times are what a gambling friend of mine would call a *dead cert*, so I'm going to take a gamble too. I'm going to give it another couple of days to make sure, and then I'm going in for the kill.

I'll set an alarm clock for 04:00, dress, pull on a pair of sneakers - which I hate wearing by the way, but needs must and all that - creep across the road, and get to work.

The caravan, besides being a fucking eyesore, will be useful insofar as it will give me shadows to lurk in, and to work in. I'm going to prise the fuel cap loose. Apparently, a guy on YouTube can do it in seconds. I've watched that video a few times, know most of it by heart, and I'm sure I can do it too. I mean, the guy isn't the smartest of people from what I've seen.

The first night, I hit a setback, because as I'm about to slink over the Cres to dart behind the caravan, a pair of foxes start copulating outside number eleven, the Security guy's house, making a right old racket. I've never heard foxes mating before, and it scares the fucking bejesus out of me, to be honest, and quite a lot of the residents of the Cres too, judging by the number of twitching curtains and anxious faces pressed up to the windows. So, the mission is aborted.

The next night, I'm back in my house by 4:32, hands shaking like an alcoholic, panting like a failed rapist, but the fuel cap lock is broken, and the alarm is blaring on the jeep - as usual.

'Job done,' I snigger in shadow.

No-one cares, no-one takes any notice, and I'm ready to put the second part of my dastardly plan into operation.

I wait forty-eight hours, until the Friday night, when the Clampetts usually have a shindig. Lots of four-by-four and bugger-off sized Beamers or Audi's parked hither and thither, rap music thumping, and lots of glass shattering in the background.

I settle down in the back bedroom until 04:00, sliding out of bed, bleary-eyed, but nerve-endings jangling, as I try to fasten buttons on my shirt, and press-studs on my jeans. My fingers are jelly, shaking, making it difficult to put my contact lenses in, but eventually coax the floppy discs over my irises. I blink several times, and once they're in place, I trundle down creaking stairs into the kitchen, and put on my trainers. The back door lets in a blast of cool air, washing away any residual cobwebs of sleep, and I clutch a litre bottle of water tightly in my fist as I stand, back to a wall, to slither along the driveway.

I peer around a corner, eyes scanning, ears straining at silence, searching for any sign of movement or sound from seventeen. There are no lights on in the house, and the curtains drawn, but there are several vehicles still at the foot of the drive, blocking a straight-line access to me.

I plot a route, between the back end of a Navara and Beamer, around the arse-end of the caravan, and up to the jeep. I sprint across the road, duck into the space, fumble with the broken lock of the fuel cap.

I hear a sound behind me and freeze, bottle of water poised at the neck of the fuel pipe.

What the fuck—?

I feel the caravan vibrating at my back, lurching and rocking as someone moves around inside. A door opens, slamming against the side panel, and the caravan lurches once more as they step down onto the drive.

Shit-shit-fucking-shitty-shit-shit.

I press against the cold panelling, holding my breath, wanting to melt, hoping not to be discovered, as footsteps head to the rear of the mobile home.

The footfalls fade into the distance, as whoever it is walks along the drive, into the road. I take a sneaky peek around a corner, in time to see a luminous hairy arse drop into view from a pair of joggers sliding to a guy's knees.

He's in front of my house, oblivious to me, fumbling at his groin. It's the big fat fucker who owns the Navara; thick, hairy, heavily-tattooed arms hanging from a white vest, bald head glinting under sodium lamps. I know what he's about to do, but can't stop it. I clench fists and jaw muscles in anger and frustration as I hear splashes of hot steaming piss spattering on soil. *Bastard!*

I've spent days rescuing plants, replacing shrubs, and adding top soil to Lena's plot, repairing damage done by the deluge and flooding caused by the tarmac dam. I even went to the trouble of saying a few prayers over it, in the hope that if there is a God, he'd bless my late wife's final resting place once more. Now, it's been defiled by some shit-for-brains chimp relieving his bloated bladder full of Bud or Heineken over it. If I could, and had both the time and the paint, I'd turn his Navara into a Cuntmobile, but as it is, I can only gaze on in apoplectic rage as he stands, legs wide apart, shaking his filthy cock over her grave.

The joggers are hoisted up around his fat, useless arse with a snap of elastic and sigh of contentment. He turns to shuffle back to the door of the caravan as the clock ticks away seconds, drawing nearer to my 4:30 deadline. I pour water into the fuel pipe, carefully place the cap back on it, and scurry between Navara and Beamer, as the caravan door slams shut, triggering the jeep alarm.

Fuck! I'm trapped!

'What the fucking hell?' a gruff voice demands from the caravan, and the door is flung open. A light comes on in the front bedroom window, hinges squeal as it opens outward, and Jethro shouts down above the din,

'Ignore it, pal. It'll reset in a minute or two.'

'Fuck that,' Baldy responds, 'Bring the bastard keys down, and we'll have a look at it.'

'What now?'

'Yes, now, you soft cunt, I told you to take it and get it fixed last week.'

The window slams annoyance, Baldy's footsteps are drawing inexorably closer, so I take the only option open to me to prevent being discovered; I grip the back bumper of the Beamer, pray it won't set off any alarm it may have fitted, slide my legs past the exhaust pipe, to squirm under it. My prayers go unheeded as the Beamer stirs from its slumbers to join in on the alarm chorus.

Someone else is roused within the mobile home,

'Fuck me gently, Jesus, you've set mine off now.'

I dare not breathe, can't move, because I'm paralysed with fear as I listen to muted voices discussing various immobilisers, and alarm systems.

It's almost 06:30 before I summon the courage to risk breaking from cover to the safety of home. I'm dithering, shivering, teeth chattering, and limbs shaking, as I close and lock the door, press my back to it, and slither to the floor. Within seconds hysteria and relief bubble up from within, and I'm laughing; laughing like a madman at the closest of close shaves I've ever had. Well, apart from the day Lena came home to collect her shopping bags, that is. Glenda and me were bollockybuff naked, hiding in the back bedroom, breathless after our role-playing.

Still, in both cases, I think it was worth it, although in hindsight, maybe the Lena situation proved the better of the two; Glenda was as hot as a docker's armpit after our near-discovery.

# Chapter Twelve

When I was talking to Winston, the black chap from number twenty-eight, in my local watering hole the other week, discussing the *Windrush* scandal, and how a lot of his generation were given shitty monikers, like Gladstone or Winston, because of old imperialistic values, I touched on the subject of irony. I mean, it's ironic that people who were subjugated or used by the Empire, saw fit to name kids after some of the most prominent exploitative figures from that time. I also mentioned it was ironic that, the day I marched up to school to defend my daughter from a tyrannical fuckwit of a teacher, is the day I started to lose the thing I loved most - after my wife, that is. He wanted me to explain. I was reticent at first, but as the night wore on, and my alcohol intake increased, I shrugged to a reflection in a toilet mirror, and thought, *what the fuck? I may as well let it all out to someone, why not this guy?*

I recounted the tale, up to the point where I bit Lena's face, and he pulled the kind of face someone might make if I'd confessed to mass murder, and that threw me a bit, but I soldiered on,

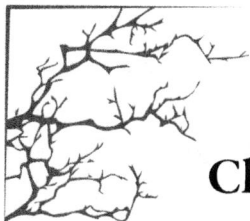

'So, when Bee sees the bite mark - which, by the way left no permanent damage or scar - she starts to ask a load of questions, as any nosy teenager might. Lena was like me in lots of ways, and she wouldn't lie to a kid, wouldn't hide facts from her own offspring, and neither would I.'

'Look, man, honesty is always the best policy with a kid, you know?' he says, taking the head off a Guinness, 'They're savvy, and they pick up on shit like that.'

'Oh, she picked up on it all right. I think she has my temper, you know? Within three or four exchanges of our differing points of view, it's turning nasty - really nasty, see?'

'What, violent?' he asks, licking foam from an upper lip, and I'm nodding slowly,

'Oh, indeedy-doody, my friend, very violent, and I'm ashamed to say it but I hoist her by the throat, up in the air as if she's a featherweight, legs kicking and pumping air as she gasps for dear life.'

'For fuck's sake, man. Your own kid?'

'Yeah,' I gasp, a lump blocking my airway.

I wish I hadn't told him. I wish I hadn't opened up to him, and picked the scab off that wound, but hey; I paved my paradise, and I put up a parking lot, as Joni Mitchell once said. She also said, *you don't know what you've lost 'til it's gone.* His eyes are glazing over with suspicion or fear, or both. I don't know, but I have to get the whole thing out to him, otherwise he'll think he's living next-door-but-one to a fucking psychopath. *Maybe he is.*

'So, then Bee and Lena get their heads together about it; whispering in the kitchen, and I go into the back garden to chill out, get some air. I don't know what kind of shit they're hatching until a few days later.'

'What happened?'

'You ever hear of Joni Mitchell, Winston?'

'Naw, man, not my cup of tea, I don't think; probably before my time too. Why?'

My eyes narrow to suspicion-filled slits,

'You don't like that Gangsta-rap stuff do you?'

He laughs and slaps the bar,

'Fuck, no. All that nigger shit? No way, man.'

I'm taken aback at a black man using the n-bomb in a crowded bar, but he finds that even funnier, so I wait for the sniggers to die down, which is a pretty poor choice of words at this moment, *but what the fuck?*

'Well, Joni Mitchell sang a song about a *Big Yellow Taxi*, see?'

'Okay, man, go on.'

'So, I'm convinced that the vehicle in question might have been more than a mere taxi.'

'Why?' he asks, finishing the dregs of brown froth.

'There's a line that goes, *and a big yellow taxi took away my old man*. Now, I know her *old man*, probably means a boyfriend, but I'm in two minds about the taxi.'

'You aren't making sense, man, just repeating. What do you think the fucking taxi is?'

'I think it's like the taxi that came to drag me away a few days after the parents' evening incident. I think that it's actually a mental health ambulance.'

His jaw drops, and his lips form a perfect silent circle of a gob-smacked, 'Oh'.

'Yeah, Lena and Bee had me sectioned, against my will, taken to a mental hospital for therapy, and a spot of counselling to smarten me up, straighten me out; stop me from being so *quick to anger*, as one said.'

'Jesus, man, that fucking sucks.'
'Oh, yes,' I giggle, 'like a fucking Electrolux.'
That one flew over his head on a 747.
No problem. I drink up, and leave him to it.

# Chapter Thirteen

I was hyped up after my struggle with Elly, wrestling her down to the cellar, flopping her onto a chair, and then using cable ties to tether the unconscious, uncooperative body in place. My limbs shook in an adrenalin rush, my mind a whirlwind of random incoherence, processing and analysing until reaching a decision. *I can't let her go. She has to die, but what do I do with the body?*

I'm thinking maybe bury it deep in the woods at the bottom of the back garden, but people walk their dogs in there at all hours of the day and night, so me digging a bloody great hole might not go unnoticed. Besides, one of the shit-factories would undoubtedly sniff it out, dig it up, and the whole fucking shebang be blown wide open.

Put it in the boot of the Cuntmobile, take it for a spin after dark to some secluded spot, maybe in an old carpet like they do in the movies? I don't have an old carpet, for a start, and the boot of a Cuntmobile is only big enough for two suitcases. Unless I fold Elly double, she won't go in there, and even then it would be a close-run thing.

I'm racking my brains to think of a way of disposing of a body that's very much alive, and I haven't decided on a method of dispatching her, let alone dumping her.

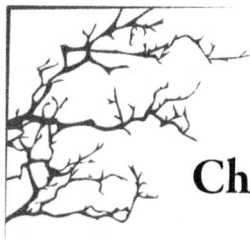

Lena always hankered for a pond in the back garden, just like her friend, Shelley, who has newts in hers, and a few frogs too, I think. I could dig a hole, deep enough for a pond, bury the body at the bottom, maybe with a hefty layer of concrete and rubble, then a plastic liner over the top, filled with water. *Why not?* No-one would dig it up. If it had newts in it, well, they're a species protected by law, aren't they? I'm fairly sure they are, so once they're in there, well...?

There are still a few hours of daylight left, and Elly's going nowhere, so I could start the work tonight. Okay, I don't have any pond liner laying around, but I could nip out in my Cunt-mobile, *I'll have to stop calling it that*, buy a roll from the garden centre tomorrow, pick up a bag of quick-setting shit they use for burying posts, *Postcrete, is it?* from the D.I.Y store on my way home. It'll only take me an hour. *Sorted, as Gordon fucking Ramsey says.*

I mark out the perimeter of the hole using loose sand, drag a spade and mattock from the back of the shed, shake cobwebs and dead spiders from the handles.

John always calls them a shovel and pickaxe, but he lives with Misery Tits, so what does he know? A pickaxe has two points, and a mattock has one, plus a cutting edge on the opposite end. A shovel has sides, whereas a spade is a flat blade. Enlightening a man like John would be too much like hard work - not as much hard work as digging a hole turns out to be though.

When we first moved into twenty-four, the back was a monoculture of grass, extending from the door to a line of trees gradually thickening to form a wooded area. Over the intervening years, we hacked away at the grass, made flower beds, paths, planted shrubs and trees to make it private. As far as I know, all the back gardens on this side of the road have been levelled; built up on the north side, using whatever came to hand to negate the effects of the one-in-ten, or maybe one-in-twelve, slope of the Cres. I've never measured it, but that's my estimate.

The previous owners were called Crapper, which we had a good chuckle over, but now the shit has hit the pan. He was a builder by trade, like Bob at number twenty, and he must have used whatever was left over from various jobs as hardcore for levelling the land. Once I'd started to dig, it wasn't long before I was unearthing house bricks, breeze blocks, and a couple of big white Belfast sinks. I don't know what they're worth, but I've put them to one side. Nostalgia has always been a thing of the past, as far as I'm concerned, but the retro look is all the rage these days, isn't it? Buy something brand new that's been made to look like it's ancient? *I'll check out the value, and stick them on eBay once Elly's put to rest.* I also found lots of large rocks, sandstone I reckon, in increasing numbers. I had a real lather on after two hours of solid digging, with an odd break for water, and a breather, and the hole was only about half the depth I wanted it to be, or thought it should be.

I'd figured maybe three feet for the pond, and another foot for the body under it. No point in going crazy. *You're already there, Stan.* I decided the large rocks will be used to decorate the perimeter of the pond to cover the liner; make it look a professional job - and a permanent one too. Shirt sleeves were caked in thick clay, my back in sweat, and smudges of filth smeared my face like war paint.

'Sounds like someone's busy,' John's voice bounced over a boundary to my left. He was trying to peer around thick shrubbery and a tree, but he'd no chance.

'Yeah, I finally decided to put a pond here. Lena used to badger me about it, but I never got around to it,' I said.

'Shame about your wife, Stan,' he said, sounding as if he really meant it, 'she'd have liked that you're doing it now though, I reckon.'

'Maybe,' I agreed, 'but it's fucking hard graft, pal.'

'Debbie keeps pestering me to make her one, but I told her how hard the soil is, and how much rubbish there is under it.'

'How'd she take that, John?' I asked, knowing full well that they had a blazing row about it, but in the end, John won his first and only victory. The coup de grâce, as I recalled was,

'Well, if you want one so bad, Debs, why not pay for someone to do it?'

As tight as a camel's cunt in a sandstorm, Misery Tits is, so John knew it was never going to happen.

'Oh, you know?' John said, 'she wasn't happy about it, but—'

I know he's shrugged his shoulder.

I wanted to say,

'When is she ever happy about anything, eh? Ever?'

Instead, I gritted my teeth, swung the mattock, and set to work, tugging and grunting, ignoring John, hoping he'd get bored, and fuck off indoors to watch Sky. I packed my tools away once it was too dark to see, but fairly confident it was as deep as it needed to be.

The next morning, I clambered into my Cun-*whoops! Nearly*, Seat, headed out to Wards' nurseries, and bought the liner. I joined the ring road to set off for Wickes, quite content. Elly had been no bother in the night, although I don't think she was best pleased at being trussed up like a Christmas turkey, to be honest. She said fuck-all when I gave her food and water before I set off, just glared at me.

I was on the home run, with four sacks of Postcrete in the boot - it was on offer, so I thought I'd buy more, and be sure I'd enough. Better looking at it than for it, eh? The liner is on the back seat of the Seat. I was tootling past a Mormon's church at the bottom of Fox Place, dodging around badly-parked cars. There was some kind of shindig going off, but I don't know if it was a wedding, Christening or whatever they call them in Mormon churches, I don't actually care. Fuck them, and Joseph Smith; they're shit at parking a car, no matter what they believe.

Anyway, as I was gliding by, I noticed a familiar pair of legs, clippety-clopping along, on perilously high heels, and wished that, like the Red Sea, I could command them to part for me. It's Glenda making her way back from the shops, looking deliciously fuckable, so I pulled over to the kerb, and offered her a lift home.

'No,' she said at first, 'it's not far from here, Stan, I can walk.'

'Don't be daft,' I said, 'jump in quick, the lights are going to change soon. It's no bother.'

She hesitated, but then slithered onto the passenger seat with a flustered sigh, and struggled with the seat belt.

'How are you these days, anyway?' she asked.

'Fine, thanks,' I said, trying to sound as normal as I possibly could with Elly tied up in my cellar, 'and you?'

'A bit fed up, to be honest,' she mumbled.

'Fed up? Why?'

She gave me a look; that look.

'I miss the old days,' she blurted out, 'you and me.'

I ignored it. She's shacked up with Bob the Builder, and we have to pretend we're only neighbours. She took the silence as her cue to elaborate,

'Bob's a nice enough bloke, but he spends most of his spare time watching footie or golf. He had the fucking cricket on the other night, gormless twat.'

'Hmm,' I grunted indifferently.

'I wish—' she started, and a hand came to rest on my thigh, but I gave her my look,

'Don't, Glenda,' I said, and she moved it.

'He never seems to see me, you know? Looks right through me most evenings; and he never wants to fu—'

'I said, don't, Glenda,' I interrupted.

She's having none of that though,

'He was as keen as mustard when we first moved in together, now he's as cold as yesterday's custard, and he's about as sexy too. I had my suspender-belt and stockings on last night and he—'

'And here we are Glenda, safe and sound,' I said with a sigh of relief, pulling on the handbrake. She slid out of the car with feline grace, fixed me with big green eyes, and said,

'Well, thanks for the lift, Stanley, but, ah, you know, if you, ah, if you ever fancy hooking up sometime soon, for a coffee or maybe, ah, well, you know?'

I parked on the drive, and unloaded my wares, with Glenda rattling around in my mind for the next hour. The coffee I don't need, but if Bob the Builder isn't delivering the goods for Glenda, I'm more than happy to oblige her on that score. Once this business with Elly is sorted, I'll put Rearender Glenda at the top of my list of things to do.

# Chapter Fourteen

The Pajero's dying, but there's nothing Jethro can do about it now. The bonnet's been up and down more times than a prostitute's panties in the last forty-eight hours, and he has his head under it again, but I can't watch the fun. A guy from Wasp Security, Alex something-or-other, lifts a mug of tepid tea to his lips, takes a healthy swig, and then continues to explain my options regarding the installation of an intruder alarm, and CCTV system.

I was going to do it myself, but when I researched it, found out how much fiddle and faff was involved, how many parts and tools were required, I thought better of the idea. Fisher. His name's Fisher. I remember it now.

He's telling me that he can install a wireless unit, in my boiler cupboard, complete with two fobs and sensors in four key positions, guaranteed to provide one hundred percent coverage in case of any unwanted guests.

'What about the basement?' he asks.

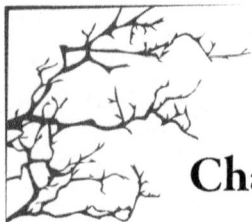

Houses on the Cres were built in the thirties, when the main domestic fuel was coal, so there was a coal hatch in front of every house where the sacks could be emptied, and the coal accumulated in a heap in the cellar. Some of them were capped off over time, but I think mine, and the one at number fifty-six, are the only ones now that aren't completely sealed, although we both have lockable metal lids over them.

'Okay,' I shrug, 'yeah, put a sensor in the cellar too.'

He makes a note on his A4 pad, and then asks,

'What about cameras?'

'Well, I only need to see the front of the house, plus the driveway, and the back garden.'

Baldy pulls up in a Navara, saunters over to Jethro, and puts his fat wrinkled, shiny head under the bonnet.

'Okie-dokie,' Alex says, 'No problem, I can site the front one near the corner of the bay window, and the rear above your bathroom window, but if I were you, I'd stick one in the basement too, just to be on the safe side.'

'Why?' I say, looking past Alex, as Baldy shakes his head, pats Jethro on the shoulder in what appears to be a form of commiseration.

'Well, the camera at the front would pick up the drive and most of the front garden, but you'd have a blind spot where the coal hatch is, even with a wide angle, see?'

I'm not really listening, but pretend to be and agree, shrugging my shoulders, adding a non-committal,

'Yeah, okay, that's fine, whatever's best.'

'Last question then,' he says draining the dregs of the tea, 'DVR or NVR, pal?'

'Sorry?' I say, perplexed by the terminology.

'Are you on the net?'

'Yes, why?'

'An NVR will let you create a network, and you'll be able to access the cameras remotely if you want to. Have you an iPad or iPhone?'

‘Phone,’ I reply, and hand it to him.

‘Sound,’ he says, and glances at my television, ‘you can view the network on your phone, or your TV, if you want?’

‘Really?’ I say, surprised but pleased by the news.

‘Oh, yeah, you’ll be able to control the lot from your phone, view it from the pub if you want, and I can set up trigger zones to let you know when someone comes near the house too.’

‘That’s great,’ I reply, and I mean it.

Once the system is installed and running, I’ll watch the Clampetts on my TV. Takeaway vans are still turning up as regular as clockwork, so that’ll be fun viewing.

Baldy is peering under the bonnet as Jethro turns the engine over, but it misfires and coughs, belching horrible sickly-coloured fumes from the rear.

Alex turns, looks across the road at the Pajero,

‘That sounds like it’s seen better days. Mind you, the Pajero’s are a pile of scrap. I prefer the Shogun, myself, but, hey-ho. That one’s definitely fucked.’

I cough to clear my throat,

‘So, how much will that lot be in total, when can you start, and how long will it take?’

‘I can fit you in this weekend; it’ll be up and running in a day, but I might have to pop back to fine-tune stuff for you. As for the price, I’ll email you a quote.’

He rises, looks at the two men working on the jeep,

‘They’re wasting their time. If they take a look at the exhaust fumes, they’d be able to tell there’s water in the fuel line, but if they keep running the engine—’

‘Will it fuck it up completely?’

'Oh, yes,' he laughs, 'definitely.'

'Oh, one last thing,' I say whilst showing him to the door, 'would it be, ah, any cheaper for cash?'

He gives me a cautious look.

'You can pay by cash, cheque or bank transfer, but it's the same price, come what may, pal.'

'But I thought-'

'You thought you'd avoid the Vodka and Tonic, if you paid cash, right?'

'Vodka and Tonic?'

'Vee-Ay-Tee,' he grins, 'VAT.'

I'm nodding like a simpleton, but what Alex says in response makes me realise I'm dealing with someone who actually has integrity; moral values, *or is it a compass?*

'No, everything goes through the books. Everything. I pay my taxes, pay my VAT, and fiddle fuck-all. Google and Amazon can cheat the system all they want, but me? I like to be straight and honest, pal.'

'Fine,' I say, 'see you on Saturday?'

'I haven't let you have the quote yet.'

'Naw,' I say waving a dismissive hand, 'just get on with it, pal.'

He thinks I'm crazy, but so does my mate Winston, in twenty-eight. Crazy, I may be, but I'm a good judge of character, and I liked the Wasp guy. He seemed honest.

I watch his black transit pulling away, revealing the empty spot where the Pajero once stood, but bald, fat and ugly is occupying the vacated space on his mobile phone. Jethro must have taken the jeep for another spin around the block.

Baldy is agitated and shouting, so I open the window a notch to hear what's going on, but he's speaking in a foreign language. It definitely isn't Mancunian or Irish, so that shoots John's theory down in flames. They still might be gypsies though.

I duck behind the curtain as his gaze gradually drifts across to my house, still listening intently.

I catch a couple of words, spat with venom during the heated conversation; *Putka, Shibanyak*, and, as he hangs up, he yells, *Chukai te!*

I'm intrigued, thumb my phone to life, and scour the internet for the words, thinking I might have to try several variations of the spellings. I get a hit on *Shibanyak* at the first search - it's Bulgarian for *fucker*. The other words are equally as vulgar, and also Bulgarian. *Putka* is pussy, and *chukai te!* means *fuck you!*

Bulgarian? I wonder. Don't get many of them around here. Well, actually, as events unfold, it turns out we do.

# Chapter Fifteen

On Saturday morning, the Wasp van is on my drive, Alex and his apprentice, Lewis, are swarming all over the house, fixing bell boxes, cameras, sensors, pulling cables to Bee's old room, where the NVR is going to be sited. I decided to put it in one of her fitted wardrobes, out of the way. I also asked him to add another camera to the job.

The rear garden camera, and the basement one, will be fine, but I decided to have an extra camera trained on the drive - and my precious Seat - and one on the front garden. Okay, it's put the price up by a couple of hundred quid, but the bonus will be a clear and unrestricted view of number seventeen's front door, drive, and side gate.

Once the burglar alarm is fitted, Alex shows me how to set and unset the panel, using either one of the fobs, or a pass code on the keypad. I select the same four digits as my bank card, so I won't forget it. He's fished the camera cables in the cavity, so there's not a single one to be seen - Fisher by name, fisher, well, you get the picture, and so did I.

He's in Bee's room with Lewis. Lewis has never set up a home camera system before, so Alex is walking him through the software for it on a laptop; instructing him, letting him enter various details, and I'm peering over his shoulder.

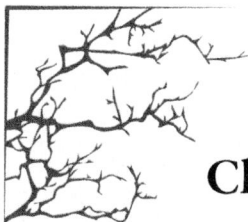

Yes, I'm a nosy bastard, but knowledge is power, and I don't want to pass up on an opportunity to learn stuff. It might come in useful at some point in the future. Picture quality is excellent. He sets up a zone around my car, so anyone approaching it will trigger an alert on my phone, and, not only can I see my car, but also Postman Pat's as well - not that I'm interested in his daily routine.

He repeats the process with my rear and front garden cameras, and by the time I hand over my cheque, I'm as au fait with the software, and passwords, as Lewis.

At 19:00 on Saturday, I'm tucking into an indecently healthy plate of homemade spaghetti, washed down with a large glass of merlot, eyes glued to my TV, as I watch the fun begin.

I'm only halfway down my list of takeaway places, but looking forward to visits from tonight's selection of unwanted hot deliveries to the Clampetts' residence. They threw me a curve ball when I first started ordering food. I watched the guy knocking on their front door, arm full of pizza boxes and two bottles of gut-rotting gunk, expecting Jethro to shake his head, refuse the delivery, and send him on his merry way. Instead, Jethro grins, and shouts over his shoulder. Elly appears, bringing cash to pay the driver. Then they slam the door, disappear inside, and must be happily munching their way through the feast. I'm miffed by this unexpected turnabout, but when the Chinese and Indian orders arrive ten minutes later, I cannot suppress my chortles of delight. There's a lot of head-shaking, and a couple of angry exchanges on the doorstep, before the drivers take the unwanted food away.

Another half hour passes, and the next batch arrives, as well as a couple of taxi's I decided to order as a bonus to the entertainment.

I've fired up the TV, tuned into my NVR, clutching my phone in one hand, and the takeaway list in the other, ready to order from Benny's Pizza, Amraj Indian Cuisine, and the Golden Palace Chinese, when a minibus draws to a halt at the kerb.

There are about eight young ladies in the vehicle, but I can't see too clearly. I know it's fairly full, and a couple of the women jump out, dressed to the nines in high heels, short skirts, and halter tops that barely contain the ample cleavage on display. It's putka on parade.

Elly totters down the driveway to whoops of delight and girlish giggling, to clamber aboard the fun bus. She's wearing a pair of white skin-tight leggings that must have been sprayed on, but end at the knees, a white scoop-neck T-shirt clinging provocatively to her titties and matching white high-heeled sandals; the ones with laces up to the calf. *Very tasty.*

I wonder where they're going, so I zoom in closer on the minibus, scanning the interior, and counting heads. If I'm honest, I have the impression that some of them are working girls; ladies of the night, but maybe that's unfair of me. These days, women don't seem to mind dressing like tarts, and flaunting their charms - which is one of the reasons I stopped drinking in the city centre, preferring to stay closer to home, and have a few beers in my local.

The driver of the minibus looks a mean bastard, with thick tattooed arms, heavy set, and thighs like the tyres of a Massey Ferguson tractor. He's fucking huge. I wouldn't want to mess with him.

The diesel creates a plume of choking black fumes as he revs the engine, and pulls away to a resounding cheer from the occupants.

I'm in two minds now whether or not to bother with the takeaway business tonight, as Jethro is in on his own, and no sign of the kid with the daft haircut, so I assume he must be at his mate's on a sleep-over or something.

I've not really been paying as much attention to their comings and goings as I should have, I suppose, but now I have a camera system up and running, I can monitor them twenty-four hours a day if I want to.

The Pajero never returned after being driven off, and the highway maintenance wagon is parked in its place next to the caravan, so I assume I really have killed the bastard, and that we'll have no more early morning alarm calls.

That puts a wry smile on my face, but I wish I could pay the twats back for Lena's memorial garden. That still rankles with me; it's festering, waiting to find focus.

Well, it isn't long before I'm presented with a golden opportunity to balance the books, settle overdue accounts, and wreak vengeance on the occupants of seventeen.

I throw the phone onto the sofa in disgust as Jethro leaves the house, dressed for a night on the town, turn off the TV, and finish the bottle of wine in a fitful sulk.

I'm so peeved that I drink a couple more bottles, and fall asleep on the sofa, snoring in a drunken stupor, until a little after midnight, when an alert on my NVR triggers, dragging me to bleary-eyed wakefulness. I peer at the tiny screen on my phone, watching as Jethro lurches up the drive to his front door, aims a key at a lock several times, before finally opening it, and falling through. Elly returns at two o'clock, rousing me once more, but by now I've managed to stumble upstairs, fall fast asleep on top of a duvet in the back bedroom.

At four-thirty, there's another trigger alert, which, at first, I think is weird, but maybe I'm conditioned to wake at that time because of the Pajero, even though I know the jeep is dead. *The jeep is dead, long live the jeep!*

I look closely at phone images, watch in fascination as the ghostly figure of Winston flickers into view by the side of the caravan. He has something in his hand, but I don't have my lenses in, I can't make out details; I just know that he's doing something in a tight space between the mobile home, and the highway maintenance van. The following morning the mystery is solved. The Clampetts, and Baldy, are gathered on the drive, pointing at the side of the caravan, so I dress quickly, and take a walk around the block, up Badger Close, and down the Cres, so I can see the graffiti. In large red letters, of what I assume to be gloss paint, he has daubed the words;

Fuck off Pikeys.

It's amusing, but not for long.

# Chapter Sixteen

I awaken in a tangle of fake-tanned limbs, black hair cascading over my face, eyes gritty, and unable to focus. I realise I must have fallen asleep with my lenses in. One arm is trapped under her, dead weight, tingling with pins and needles as circulation resumes. My tongue is furred over, garlic and stale lager, bright light stabbing eyeballs from a hundred-watt bulb overhead, dangling from flex, my body cold on one side, covered in goose pimples, but the warmth of her nakedness delicious at the other.

I slide free of the entwining embrace, trying not to wake her, but failing, as cuffs rattle against the pipe work, and she emits a low groan of frustration. I echo the moan as I realise what a dreadful mistake I'd made last night. Eyelids flicker to reveal accusing blue eyes, and I know that maybe she thinks it was a mistake too.

I don't know what to say to her, as I stand to pull on discarded clothing, slightly damp and ice cold. I should have brought a duvet down with the mattress.

'What time is it?' she husks, in what I now know is a thick Bulgarian accent. I shrug, peer at my phone,

'Almost half-past eight, why?'

'They will come soon, and we will both die.'

'How do you know that? Why will we both die?'

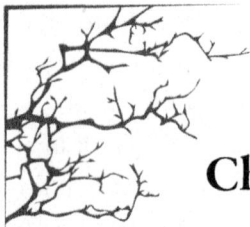

'They will think I betrayed them, informed on them, and you must die to cover their tracks.'

I rub my face with both hands.

This isn't making sense.

She laughs,

'You still don't understand, do you, Stan?'

'No,' I reply honestly, 'I haven't got a clue—'

'How do you think I came to your country? Why do you think I'm here?'

'I don't fucking know, you wouldn't tell me.'

'No, but now it's too late.'

'How is it too late? Betrayed who?'

'The gangsters and slave-traders; Bulgarian Mafia.'

What? She's kidding.

'You don't believe me? Ha! You'll see. We'll die.'

The look on her face tells me she's deadly serious, as she pulls legs under her, wraps arms around shoulders to warm her nakedness rather than hide it.

'I'll be back,' I say as I head for the stairs to fetch her some clothing from Bee's wardrobe. Elly's won't be dry yet, and I'm sure there'll be something in there that she can wear. I'm guessing, but I reckon she's more or less the same size as Bee was when she left home.

'Fetch my phone please, Stan. We may be able to buy some time.'

I select a pair of blue jeans, white bra and panties, a red *Linkin Park* T-shirt, detour through the kitchen to pick up the iPhone from the worktop. I notice she's had missed calls, and dozens of messages, but the phone's locked so I can't scroll through them. The ones on the screen are in Bulgarian anyway.

I hand her the bundle of clothing, and the phone, but she ignores the garments in favour of finding out what's been happening in the outside world.

'Kopele!' she says, slamming a fist onto a knee, and then looking up at me, eyes blazing, 'they're searching for me, threatening that if I don't come back with the money, they will find me, and kill me.'

'What money? Who's Kopele?'

She grins,

'Kopele is my word for your English *bastard*, but the money is what I owe them for my passage to this country. It is several thousand pounds now.'

'You're joking?'

I can tell she isn't, and I'm getting twitchy.

'If they look at the camera footage, they will see me coming here; they will know I am here.'

'Camera footage? What camera footage?'

'When the jeep was sabotaged, and the caravan was painted, Prase installed a camera at the house.'

'Who is Prase? Your boyfriend or husband?'

She laughs again.

'No, Prase means *pig*. He's what you call a pimp, and he lives with me to make sure I do as I'm told.'

Jethro the pig? That's funny. What about the kid?

'So, who's the kid?'

'He's my son, and he's what they call *insurance*, it's a long story, but we don't have time, we must leave.'

'Leave?' I shriek, 'I'm not going anywhere, lady, and neither are you. Hand me the phone.'

'What? Why?'

'Just hand me the phone, and maybe I can manage to save us both. Can you access the cameras on this?'

'Yes.'

'Good,' I say distractedly, as nervous fingers flit over the surface of her phone. *I just hope I can do this in time.* As I'm working, I realise why Elly came hammering on my door - she's seen recorded footage of me in action.

# Chapter Seventeen

I'm walking along Heathfield Lane, which I used to refer to as Jimmy's Lane, because Heathfield is similar to Hetfield, and James Hetfield is guitarist with Metallica. My therapist and counsellor advised me to stop listening to heavy metal music in an effort to keep anger in check, but I don't think it did squat. Well, aside from robbing me of one of my simple pleasures that is.

I'm whistling a riff from *Enter Sandman*, imagining a grinding guitar churning it out, as James Hetfield's gravel voice barks the infectious lyric in my head.

Suddenly, a large Dalmatian dog is bounding toward me, tongue lolling and tail wagging. I freeze in my tracks. I hate dogs, and they hate me. I don't trust them, and they can smell fear oozing from my pores. I personally view them as walking shit factories, where food goes in one end, they run around for a while, and then shit flies out of the other end. They serve no purpose as far as I can tell, other than fouling pavements or common land.

Winston rounds the corner, shouting the dog's name, which may be Pixie, or Trixie, but I don't give a flying fuck what it's called. Dogs in general are a nuisance and a source of terror for me, but Dalmatians are highly strung creatures, prone to unpredictability; masters of chaos, and this one is a champion.

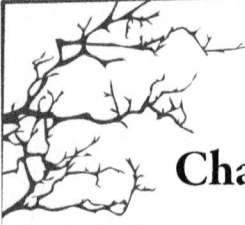

The damned thing circles me several times, jumping up; tail wagging, licking and shaking as though it's taking a massive shit. Some say that, in reality, there are no bad dogs, simply bad owners who don't train or look after their charges properly, but they've never stared down the loaded muzzle of a Pit Bull Terrier, or into the salivating maw of a Rottweiler. They've never trembled under the alerted gaze of a Doberman or a German Shepherd that's decided the smell of pure fear emanating from me is the signal that I'm lunch.

Fortunately, Winston closes the gap quickly, wraps a choke lead around the beast's neck, and brings it to heel,

'Are you off to the pub, Stan, my man?' he grins.

'Yeah, nothing like a few pints of an evening.'

'Too right, man. Mind if I join you?'

'Be my guest, Tony, I think I owe you one anyway.'

Winston likes his friends to call him *Tony*, because, he says, it makes him sound less like a nigger. Go figure. I'm fine with it.

'Aw, man, you should've seen your face,' he laughs.

'When? Just now?'

'Yeah, man, I honestly thought you were going to shit your pants back there.'

'I, ah, I don't like dogs, Tony. I don't trust them.'

'Mine's as daft as they come, she'd never hurt—'

'Anyone? Yeah, all dog owners say that, usually just before one of the bastards bites me.'

'No way, Stan,' the grin remains fixed, as he pushes through into the bar, the dog sliding under a table in one corner, the barmaid frowns,

'You know you aren't s'posed to bring her in here, Tony,' she rumbles, arms folding over her ample, almost over-spilling, bosom.

'Aw, come on, Tina, she's no bother.'

'Well, if the landlord sees her—'

'All right, if he comes in, I'll leave.'

I order a couple of Guinness, as Tony commandeers seats at the table where the dog is lying. I'm still eyeing the hound warily, convinced the slavering monster, with sharp, fanged teeth and claws wants to eat me, to rend me, tear me limb from limb with powerful jaws, to crush my bones, and grind them to powder.

I look away; try to distract my mind with a decision about whether to have pork scratchings or crisps, maybe a pack of salted, or dry-roasted, nuts.

'Give us a pack of dry-roasted peanuts, please, Tina, and get yourself a drink.'

'Not tonight, Stan, I'm in the car, but thanks for the offer all the same.'

I shout over to Tony,

'You want any snacks, pal?'

'No thanks, man, just the black stuff.'

I slide into a chair opposite, rip open the foil packet, and heft a few nuts into my mouth, wash them down with a gulp of ice-cold nectar.

'They always keep the Guinness well here,' I say, as I wipe a foam moustache from my upper lip, 'a lot better than across the road at the Forester's.'

'Hmm,' Tony agrees around the rim of the glass.

'I'm glad I bumped into you anyway, Tony. I've been meaning to ask, what do you make of the new folks who moved into number seventeen?'

'What, the Pikeys?'

'Are they Pikeys?' I counter, 'I don't know.'

'Why else would they have the caravan on the drive? They're Irish fucking travellers, man; Pikeys.'

'The Pajero's gone at last though,' I say priming him, getting him ready for another question or two, before I tell him what I know.

'Oh, God, yeah, man. Like, was I ever glad to see the back of that pile of fucking scrap, waking me up at half-past bastard four every morning? Why didn't he get it seen to?'

'I don't know, but it's gone now.'

'Good riddance too. I hope the caravan goes next.'

I swirl foam into a head on my drink, squint down at it, as if in thought,

'Did you see the graffiti on the side of it?' I ask.

Tony fidgets in his seat, and I've never seen a black man blush until tonight, but there's definitely more colour in his cheeks as he looks at me sideways,

'Yeah, man, looks like someone else hates them too, eh, Stan?'

'Hmm. Did I tell you about the new camera system I had installed over the weekend?'

'No. Why'd you have that done?'

I tell him about the tarmac ramp, about Lena's grave, and he coos sympathy and understanding. Then I press on with details of the vandalism to my car, the defiling of the grave for a second time by Baldy. All to explain why I had a burglar alarm and CCTV system fitted. I even show him pictures on my phone.

'Looks good, man,' he grins, 'how much did it cost?'

When I tell him, he whistles through his teeth, like a mechanic who realises that the guy who owns the broken down car knows fuck-all about it, and makes that noise to cover up or justify the rip-off about to happen.

'Well worth it though,' I say.

'Yeah-yeah, man,' Tony agrees.

'Do you, ah, do you know what she does for a living? Only, I know he works for the highways department, but I've no idea what Elly May does to earn a crust.'

'You know her name, man?'

'Naw, I call her that because, well, let me get you a fresh pint, and then I'll explain, eh?'

'I'll get these, Stan, you got the first ones.'

I insist, badger him into letting me buy two more, and then I tell him about the Clampetts. By the time I finish, he's slapping a thigh, giggling like a big girl's blouse, and I'm worried that he might actually piss his pants.

When he's finally calmed down enough, he tells me she works at the hairdressing salon, along the main road, near the Mormon's church - but he doesn't know what they call them, or what goes on in them either.

'Is she full-time or part-time?' I ask.

'Full-time, I think, Stan, why?'

'Oh, no reason, just curious, that's all.'

'My wife, Jules, goes there for her split-end trimming and tickling once a fortnight; she says she's a nice enough sort, but has a funny kind of accent. I told her it's because she's a fucking Pikey, but Jules won't believe me.'

'Yeah, women are funny like that,' I say.

'How'd you mean?'

'Well, no matter what I'd tell Lena, or Bee for that matter, they'd hardly ever take it at face value. It used to drive me nuts.'

To emphasise my point, I swallow another handful of dry-roasted, but one catches in the back of my throat, and Tony has to wallop my back a few times to dislodge it. I rinse it away with the last of my Guinness.

'You want another one for the road, my man?' Tony says, already rising to his feet to go to the bar. I don't want to refuse, because I'm actually enjoying my night out, and I haven't sprung my surprise on him yet.

He toddles back to the table with the top-ups, places them on soggy beer mats, and slides onto his seat.

'Cheers, Tony; always a pleasure, never a chore.'

'Did you see the minibus full of skirt the other night, Stan?'

'Oh, yes, I had a really good look at it later, when I played back the footage on my CCTV system. You've no idea how much you can see with this thing. I could zoom in on quite a lot of the action too.'

'I'll have to get one of those fitted at the kennels,' he says.

'Kennels?'

'Yeah, me and Jules run a boarding kennel, not far from the city limits, that's what we do for a living.'

'Does it pay well?'

'Better than working for some other schmuck, and we get a lot more free time to do what we want. The bonus is the quar-antined animals - they have to be kept isolated for four months if the owners haven't done their homework and had the pets inoculated properly.'

'Are there many like that?'

'Oh, you'd be surprised, Stan, but we can also add a few bob onto the vet's bills. It pays really well then.'

'I couldn't do it, Tony.'

'Well, obviously, if you don't like dogs—'

'Naw, it's cleaning up all the shit, feeding them, and walking the bastards I couldn't cope with.'

'We employ kennel maids for that, man, you know? They're mostly minimum wage girls, fresh out of school, who just like to be around animals. They'd do it for fuck-all if they could - not that we'd exploit them.'

'So, what do you charge per week?'

'Prices start at £15.50 per day for something like, say a Chihuahua, plus VAT, but then there are loads of extras we can stick on there too. Overnight stays, or the luxury kennel option bring in a fair bit of cash, and we charge for bathing, and walking too. It's a fucking license to print cash, Stan.'

'Cats?'

'Well, obviously cats are smaller, so the price goes down, but not by much. Pity you don't like dogs though, my friend.'

'Why?' I ask.

'Well, we're expanding the business, putting up more cages, and so on. Jules said we ought to have an on-site manager to oversee things, you know? Save us having to keep driving over there every day to organise stuff, keep an eye on the staff.'

'What? You think I'd be suitable?'

'Hey, man, there's a beautiful flat above the offices, and it's quiet - no fucking Pikeys neither. You can use a computer, can't you?'

'Well, yeah, of course I can.'

'You're out of work, aren't you?'

'Yeah, although I've got a few quid in the bank, left over from when the insurance policy paid out on Lena, but—'

Tony shrugs, downs the rest of his drink,

'No worries, man, if it's not for you, well, it's not for you, I'm not pressurising you into it. Anyway, I'd better go, pal.'

'Have a squint at this before you go, Tony.'

I wasn't going to show him, not after he'd offered me a job with accommodation thrown in, but I wanted to see the look on his face. I couldn't resist the temptation.

He peers at the phone screen as I play footage of him daubing graffiti on the side of the caravan, and a guilty expression creeps across his face,

'Fuck, man,' he says, and then looks at me, 'you, ah, you aren't going to show anyone that are you?'

I'm giggling,

'Of course not, pal. I'm going to delete it, right now. Before your very eyes, see? It's gone; never existed.'

He breathes a sigh of relief,

'Thanks. I gotta go.'

As he turns to leave, I grin again,

'Hey, Tony? Fuck the Pikeys, right?'

# Chapter Eighteen

It's fashionable, almost compulsory nowadays, to be afflicted by mental illness, whether you're a celebrity or a member of the royal family. They bleat from the pages of tabloids, and women's magazines, about their battle with alcoholism, depression, bi-polar disorders or anorexia and bulimia. Back in the early nineties, when I was detained under Section 2 of the Mental Health Act for twenty-eight days, people weren't so cool about it. They wouldn't slap your back, tell you it was okay, or understand any of the shit being heaped upon your shoulders.

My former employers were the same. They couldn't quite get to grips with one of their loyal and, up to that point, diligent, hard-working members of staff being not right in the head, and needing treatment. I don't think Bee or Lena was happy about it either, but I forgave them, in the end, after my release.

What made things worse was the continued care, and counselling afterward. It was like being on probation. I'd have to show up each week to listen to a load of bollocks, answer questions - stupid questions - about my frame of mind, if I had any temptation or propensity for self-harm.

I had a fucking list of all the cunts I wanted to harm, but I wasn't on the list, and neither were Lena and Bee.

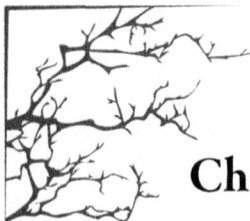

Farty Lil, the woman in number thirty, was promoted to top of that list. Why? She was one of my clinicians at the institute, pumping me full of drugs, making me pop pills on a daily basis, being supercilious and smarmy, but suffering from acute flatulence. She'd let it rip, no matter where she was or what she was doing. Noisy, smelly farts that rippled in her panties, causing choking clouds of gas.

She'd do it at the crowded bus stop too. She had no shame or compunction; she never looked around, never checked to see if the coast was clear. Nope. She should have been in a live-action version of *Frozen*, cast as Elsa, because she certainly knew how to *Let it Go.*

I was surprised to see her moving in up the road from me, and miffed by it too. Having a constant reminder of my days; incarcerated against my will, drip-fed drugs, and spoon-fed bullshit. The dopey twat can't even be bothered to keep her garden in some semblance of tidiness either. She never cuts the privet hedge, so it sprawls over onto the pavement every summer, forcing pedestrians onto the road, and don't get me started on her back garden. There's a *Photinia, Red Robin*, romping away, as well as apple, and cherry trees that are in serious need of pruning. Fuck me, what an eyesore.

I can only see the top of them from my back bedroom window, but I shudder to think what the rest of the garden looks like. I hate neglect. It's criminal. At least John and Misery Tits make an effort with theirs.

'So, what do you like to do in your spare time, Mister Mortimer?' she asked me, and I was tempted to tell her,

'Cat-strangling and masturbation, but not at the same time.'

Of course, I didn't say that. I might've been insane, but I wasn't fucking stupid.

'I like to watch films, read the occasional book, and listen to music, but sometimes do the odd repair job, you know? D.I.Y. That sort of thing, why?'

'What genre of film?'

'Oh, anything from science fiction to crime thrillers, and maybe the odd horror movie thrown in.'

'I don't think horror movies would be very good for you at the moment, Mister Mortimer.'

I wanted to do a Hannibal Lector, and bite the bitch's face off, but I did that with Lena and look where it landed me.

'Okay,' I shrugged indifferently.

'And books?' she pressed.

I hadn't the heart to name Stephen King, or Thomas Harris, for fear of a similar rebuttal, nor Dean Koontz for that matter, although his last couple of books were crap, to be honest.

'I think the last book that I read was, ah, *The White Plague*, by Frank Herbert,' I lied. I read that several years ago, but I wasn't telling her. She asked me to give her a synopsis of it, which I did, and she decided that wasn't for me either, the cow. If she'd had her way, I'd be back to *Janet and John*.

'What about your music collection?'

Okay, I know I should've seen it coming, but I love music, love it to bits, and I wasn't going to lie about what I listened to. I mean, music's a personal thing, like an extension of the soul, you know?'

'Metallica, Judas Priest and Budgie—'

'Budgie?' she asked, incredulously, 'Adam Faith?'

'No,' I sighed impatience, 'they're a three-piece rock band from Tredegar in Wales.'

'Like Metallica?' she asked. *She hadn't a clue.*

'Metallica did a cover version of Budgie's *Breadfan.*'

'So, they're similar?'

'Yes,' I hissed, red mist descending.

'Well, what I'd like you to do, Mister Mortimer, is to listen to more melodic, soothing things, perhaps Enya or maybe even some Marvin Gaye; something to keep your mind in a placid state. Yes?'

Enya? Marvin fucking Gaye? That is gay. Totally.

Around and around the questioning went, pointless and endless, increasingly annoying, and I couldn't wait to get out of that hell hole. I played their game, pretended to be good; the model patient, with a soppy grin, and all the right answers to the dopey fucking questions to gain me remission. I had to toe the line after release, attend counselling every week and keep a diary - which I always lied in - just to let them think they'd tamed me, but they hadn't. They never would.

When I returned to work, the Human Resources team was as bad, asking me if I was okay, if this was the right time for me to return so soon after my, ah, illness. Dance around the daffodils and tiptoe through the tulips all you want, but I know where this is heading. They were upset, and sympathised with me, but still fed me a crock of shit to justify getting rid of me.

'Some of your co-workers aren't comfortable around you, Mister Mortimer, and there's also a problem with the amount of time you're absent for, ah, treatment, is it?'

Yeah, well. The other night, I caught the tail-end of one of those superhero movies, *Avengers Assemble* I think it was, and someone asks this big bloke if he needs to get angry to turn green, and smash shit. I didn't understand it all because I'd missed most of it, but he turns around and grins,

'That's my secret, Captain, I'm always angry.'

Yeah, well so am I, and I fucking love it. I'm like the strings of a guitar, I suppose. If I'm too slack, all you'll get is a farty noise, you know? Tuneless vibrations. If I'm too tight, well, I snap. Most of the time, I'm wound tight enough to keep adrenalin flowing, pumping into my brain, allowing me to think, and function, on a level normal for me. I've never confused *normality* for *ordinary*, because when you come right down to the nitty-gritty, normality has never been standardised or quantified. Ordinary has though, and I don't want to be ordinary, see? *No chance.*

Besides which, Rearender Glenda liked a little crazy now and again.

# Chapter Nineteen

I packed in with the Takeaway Torment. It became so boring in the end that I lost interest. In fact, the only thing that does keep me glued to my monitor is the minibus full of putka once a fortnight, and a tidy-looking woman who turns up in a silver Astra every Tuesday, with what looks to me like a portable massage table. I can only surmise that either Jethro or Elly are getting a regular rubdown, or one of them is learning how to do it.

I have my regular night at the local with Tony, where we put the world to rights, and have a couple of beers, but he told me that the Clampetts have bought a dog. He says they bought it after the caravan was painted, and daubed with graffiti. Tony's still worried I might bubble him for the dastardly deed, and I keep teasing him about it, but I haven't seen hide nor hair of a dog, if you'll pardon the expression. They never take it for a walk, according to Tony, and it seems to stay in the house most of the time, gazing out of the bay window. Again, I've never seen it.

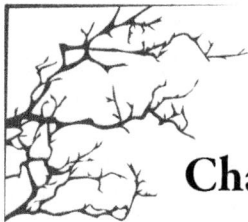

This morning I heard it though, as I've heard it every morning for the past week; yap-yap-fucking-yap. Then a dog on Badger Close joins in. It's a regular routine. Jethro comes out of the house at six-thirty, jumps in the highway maintenance van, revs the engine for two minutes, before roaring off down the Cres in a cloud of blue smoke. The Hound of the Baskervilles is baying for blood at exactly seven-thirty, and thirty minutes later, Elly May appears, as the canine cacophony is silenced. She has a fag at the kerb, waiting for a taxi to arrive, and then she disappears for the day. In the distance, I can faintly hear the sound of a dog yapping, so I assume the poor shit factory's either locked in the kitchen, or in one of the bedrooms, but I've never seen it, just heard it.

I'm not losing any shut-eye from it, as I'm usually up and around by seven-thirty, or maybe a quarter-to eight at the latest, but the noise irritates me, grates on my nerves. It's actually worse than foxes shagging, or cats getting up to shenanigans in the back garden, triggering my alarm.

I might get an air-rifle and sort the bastards out once and for all. Then I consider the likely outcome. If I shoot any of the neighbourhood cats, or the shit factory across the road, then they'll be taken to the vet's, a pellet found, and I'll be up shit's creek without a paddle. Someone is bound to put two and two together.

The police may even be involved, so I decide a better strategy has to be devised to silence the fucker for good. I begin researching pet welfare on the net, and find out that not only do dogs love the taste of it, but anti-freeze is as deadly as a bullet to the brain for them. It's probably the number one pet-killer out there, and I've a full bottle of it in the boot of my Seat.

I could use rat-killer or slug bait, but they won't be as fast-acting, or reliable, as anti-freeze. Apparently, it's the ethylene glycol they can't resist once they taste it, so I reckon if I dose up a nice juicy steak for Bonzo across the road, he'll gulp it down.

A page on the internet reckons a fraction under three ounces, 88 millilitres, will do the job. When I check this amount in a measuring jug, it looks like too much volume to be able to lace a steak with. I have to re-think the plan to come up with a better delivery method.

I'm in the back bedroom on the computer, looking for other ways to poison the damned thing, when John lets Charlie out onto the back for his morning constitutional dump. Charlie's an old white Highland Terrier, as soft as a brush, and the only dog, besides Tony's, disinterested in taking lumps out of me. He lets me pet him, and he never barks or causes any bother. Okay, he's old, but he's a shit factory, and I still don't think I'd ever want one as a pet.

John throws a ball for Charlie to fetch, and ancient little legs pump as he waddles after it, short tail wagging like crazy as he brings the ball back.

Sometimes though, Charlie will hold onto it, chew it a few times, before dropping it at his master's feet. That's when I hit on the idea - the solution.

I'll fill a tennis ball with anti-freeze using a syringe, heft it into the back garden of number seventeen, and let a canine's curiosity, and animal instincts, do the job for me.

I only have to wait until the fur-ball is out and about, barking and creating a din - and I know exactly when that will be. *Every dog has its day,* I giggle.

The caravan was towed away the other day by the fat Bald bloke who pissed on my garden. He rolled up in his Navara, hitched the *Fuck off Pikeys* mobile home to the rear, and it hasn't been seen since. Either it's been sited on a permanent pitch somewhere, or they've chipped it in for some cash, but my money, and theirs, is on the latter option. If I owned a caravan site, I wouldn't want that eyesore cluttering the place up. *No way.*

The mobile home's departure means I'll have nothing to hide behind when I throw a sodden ball over the fence.

# Chapter Twenty

Americans call it soccer, the English, football, but I call it a load of bollocks. I take issue with Karl Marx on this too. He's quoted as saying that *"religion is the opiate of the masses"*. The trouble is, he's misquoted, because the full text of his speech, states; *"Religion is the sigh of the oppressed creature, the heart of a heartless world, and the soul of soulless conditions. It is the opium of the people"*. I don't doubt for a minute that religion may be what Marx claimed it to be then, but these days, football is the faith, Messi or Ronaldo the new Messiah, and for all I know, Gareth Southgate could be the second coming. It's still a load of shite.

Most Saturday's I see hordes of football fans, which is an abbreviated form of *fanatic* - a person filled with an excessive and single-minded zeal - gathering in the city centre for pre-match male bonding, excessive drinking, and generally unruly or obnoxious behaviour.

They've shelled out their hard-earned cash on shirts, programs and tickets to watch twenty-two overpaid twats kick a sack of wind around for ninety minutes. I can never understand how people can endure it each week.

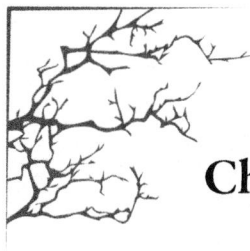

How cunts like Gary Lineker, Wayne Rooney, or that other gormless shit-for-brains with the anorexic bimbo of a wife, Beckham? Is it Beckham? Yeah, maybe, but how, and why, have they been elevated to their current status, and why can't the loonies who watch the game realise that they're keeping these clowns in a style, and manner, that they can only dream of? *Sometimes manor houses too.*

The church used to do exactly the same with the poor ignorant masses; fleece them of cash to live high on the hog, and have palaces and churches built on the backs of the willing. All on the basis that it would get them a few Brownie points in the hereafter. What a con.

Most of the time, I pay no heed to any of it, but I've noticed an increase in the number of St George's Cross flags flying on cars travelling up and down the Cres. Then the penny drops. It's summer, and it's 2018, so it must be time for a World Cup competition again. *Oh, my fucking God;* that means Lineker'll be ramping up the rhetoric, bleating about 1966, and how we could win it this year. Frank Skinner will be rolling in cash from the royalties as *Three Lions* drones on. That professional Jew he knocks around with. *David Baddiel?* He'll be rubbing his hands with glee too.

I've been immersed in the daily life of Clampetts, so I haven't been keeping up to speed with much else. I've monitored the minibuses, lads' nights out, sleep-overs for the kid with the shitty haircut. I've even giggled as Elly May trundled a wheelie bin to the kerbside in her pyjamas and fluffy slippers.

I'm driving back from a weekly shopping expedition to a local supermarket, wondering why there's no queue at the checkout, why roads are so empty, why it's so quiet on the estate.

I don't know In-ger-land, as the ignorant masses like to chant, is playing Sweden, or that it's an afternoon kick-off. I certainly don't know the Clampetts will use it as an excuse to invite all their gormless fucking mates around, to clutter the Cres with badly-parked vehicles, to party the afternoon away, as they drink copious amounts of alcohol.

I have to manoeuvre around a double-parked Beamer and Audi to ease onto my drive. As I nudge the nose of the Seat onto Postman Pat's, and I'm wrestling the stick into reverse, another big black four-by-four hurtles around a bend from Badger Close, screeching to a halt in a plume of burnt rubber only inches from the side of my car.

It's Baldy, in his Navara, glaring at me through the windscreen, mouthing obscenities at me, gesticulating. I only know what happens next because Tony tells me all about it, in gruesome detail; after the police have taken witness statements, after the hospital releases me, and the hoo-ha dies down. Tony is walking the dog, and comes around the corner, just as the action starts.

Baldy is impatient; the Sweden game is only minutes away from kick-off, and he wants to grab a front row seat on a sofa in the Clampetts' lounge, wrap his meaty fist around the neck of a Bud to chant and cheer. He's revving the engine, bouncing the jeep nearer the side of my car on the brake and accelerator, shouting, shaking his fist.

I jump out of the car; skirt around the rear end to ask the gorilla what his fucking problem is, why he can't wait a God-damned minute for me to reverse onto my drive. He responds in a mixture of Bulgarian, and English, yells that I'm taking too long about it, screaming shibanyak and putka at me.

For some reason there's an old Rolling Stones song rattling around in my head, and I can't shake it, or silence the lyric, and flashes of memory of a concert, long ago.

Mick Jagger is bounding around on stage, audience wild and raucous as inner-tube lips pout, hands clapping in time to pelvic thrusts and gyrations,

"Everywhere I hear the sound of marching charging feet, boy, 'cause summer's here and the time is right for fighting in the street, boy."

Then I see the red mist descend, and the memory of a fat luminous hairy arse, as he pisses on Lena's grave. I tell him to get fucked as I draw closer to the Navara, but he's as angry as I am, and in no mood to listen.

Colour suffuses the jowly face, distorting in a rage to match my own as he shuffles in the leather seat.

He opens the door - a heavy black gate, from which a monster is about to emerge - but I'm not going to wait for that to happen. As he steps down, half-in and half-out of the frame, I push the door back, throwing my bulk behind it to trap him, making him drop the knife.

*A knife!* My mind screams in outrage.

I grab the handle of the door to pull it open a fraction, and then slam it back on him, again and again.

'Pull a fucking knife on me, will you?' I yell, 'Pull a knife? On me? Fuck you!'

Bang! Bang! Bang!

He slithers to the floor, groaning, but making a grab for the weapon. I kick him in the guts, and then slam the door on his bald, fat-rolled head and neck.

Bang!

'I'll teach you to pull a fucking blade on me!'

Bang!

'I'll teach you, putka!'

I don't know how much damage has been caused to his tiny Neolithic brain, or care, as my spittle splashes a blotchy face surrounding eyes that are rolling in sockets, teetering on the verge of consciousness.

He looks like Glenda's ex-husband Derek did after I'd sorted him out. There's a look in the unfocused eyes; a sort of comprehension that this hasn't gone according to plan, that something unexpected has happened, that he's fucked with the wrong guy.

Well, he's definitely fucked with the wrong guy this time all right; just like Derek did when he found out about our affair.

'What's the matter, Derek?' I leer into Baldy's face, 'Not used to anyone standing up to you? Thinking you're such a big tough fucking hombre, eh?'

The commotion is attracting a lot of attention, and a lot of anxious faces peer through windows, or open doors, to see more clearly. Postman Pat is on the drive, gawping. Misery Tits and the Security guy are silhouettes, framed in their doorways. Tony is approaching, a daft black and white dog barking, straining at the leash, as guests at the Clampetts' lurch into the road, shouting and encouraging Baldy to fight back.

His head is split at the temple, blood is oozing from a ruined nose, and he's gasping for breath, hand trembling over the handle of the blade.

I stand on the hand, hearing the crepitus grinding of a broken wrist under my instep, relish the sound and feel of damage I'm inflicting as I kick the weapon aside.

I slam the door on him a couple more times, watch the lights go out, let the adrenalin shakes subside, laughter bubbling up within, but I feel cleansed; vital. The beauty of rage is exquisite, even during the aftermath, when the hysterical giggles threaten to overwhelm me. It's almost like post-orgasmic chill, when you've fucked like rabbits, and lay panting and exhausted on a bed, bathed in sweat and passion.

The green guy's voice echoes in my head,

'That's my secret, Captain, I'm always angry.'

Elly May must have been in the garden, because she saunters through the gate in slippers and pyjama bottoms to see what the racket is about.

I find the sight of her so funny I collapse in a fit of uncontrollable laughter, almost to the point of tears, until Tony's hand comes to rest on my shoulder,

'Hey, Stan, my man, come on. Leave him, he's had enough.'

'Yeah,' I grunt, chest heaving, 'had enough.'

I think Glenda must've called the coppers. A distant wail of sirens echoes on the heat of a summer's day, but I don't hear them. I don't hear any of it. I'm even unaware of the brindle Staffordshire terrier hurtling toward me. It jumps up at me, clamping meaty jaws around my arm, as I stagger back under its bulk, teeth rending flesh.

The tetanus jab leaves my buttocks numb, and a daft copper tries telling me that the dog can't be put down. It isn't covered by the Dangerous Dog Act of 1991. No-one is pressing charges, which I don't understand at the time, but obviously realise why later, when the plan to poison the dog is put into action, and I end up with Elly May in my cellar, a prisoner.

# Chapter Twenty-One

Being in the hospital brings back unhappy memories. The antiseptic smell; patients, shambling in white gowns gaping at the rear, wandering to exits for a cigarette, or a breath of fresh air, all dredge up the past.

Lena, looking pale, tiny in a huge bed, tubes in her flesh, and drips by her side, a sickly yellow cast to a once rosy complexion, almost breaks my heart.

Oh, Lena. Dear sweet, Lena, how has it come to this? Why has it come to this?

Pancreatic cancer is an old folks' disease, the doctor told me; not one a vibrant, loving and energetic woman in her forties should have, which is why it wasn't diagnosed in time to save her; until it was much too late.

She'd complain from time to time about back pain, or aches in her stomach, but put it down to her workload, and sometimes blamed it on indigestion. Occasionally, it would keep her awake at night, but she'd started losing weight, and feeling sick, having to jump out of bed in the night to go to the bathroom and vomit. There'd be shivers when she thought she was coming down with a flu virus, and she'd take a few days off work, stay in bed with a hot drink, and Paracetamol or Ibuprofen.

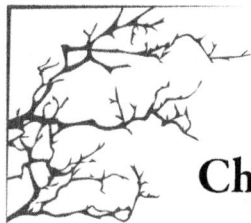

I'd been fired by then, so I spent my free time doing household chores; cleaning, cooking, ironing, and loading the washing machine. If the weather was fine, I'd hang the stuff out in the garden, if it rained, the tumbler would be fired up. I was absorbed, engrossed, and never gave it a second thought.

I first met Lena through a friend of a friend, after a trip to Jersey in eighty-seven. Lena had left home, after an argument with her elder brother, to live with grandmother on the island for the summer, which, having met him, I could easily understand. I'd move to Timbuktu to be free of his hypochondriac moaning.

Claire, the friend of a friend in question, was a tall lady in her late teens, and wouldn't have looked out of place on an adult dating site. I could've imagined her posing for a camera, dressed in a figure-hugging Basque, perilously high heels shining with a dazzling glare, fishnet stockings and suspender belt, using a pseudonym, like Dominatrix Desire. Her profile would be accompanied by various stern-looking photographs of her, resplendent in Goth-style make up. She would have black hair and eyes that were liberally coated over with mascara, like Dusty Springfield or Alice Cooper, but with vivid red, glossy pouting lips. *Come here, you snivelling toad, and let me dig my heels in you.*

Despite her intimidating outward appearance, and her obvious gaucheness, Claire was actually a good girl, and worked in Jersey for the summer in a busy hotel, along with several of her friends, and had the additional luxury of accommodation provided free of charge.

Over drinks in a late night bar prior to her departure, she suggested that her boyfriend, Stephen, and I join her on the island, and use one of the spare rooms at the place she was staying. On the strength of this drunken debate, a ferry was booked, which included the cost of transporting Stephen's car. This meant that we wouldn't pay parking charges on the mainland in our absence, and would be able to drive around the island once there. We split the cost of fuel, and Stephen drove to the south coast to meet the ferry well in advance of the sailing time.

Claire met us as we disembarked, an anxious frown creasing her brow, and making her look a little too stern.

Dominatrix Desires was displeased, and I knew that the fat had hit the shin from the offset. She clambered into the car, cursing her size, long legs, and the fact that she had bad news to impart; really bad news. She took one huge lungful of fresh Jersey air and said,

'So, my supervisor said that there's no way she'll let a couple of blokes from the mainland stay in one of the spare rooms. They could get up to all kinds of antics, and damage things, and then scoot off back without paying a cent towards the cost of repairs.'

She saw the anxious exchange of glances between us,

'Don't worry though, because I've had a word with my friends at the hotel, asked around for you to get you fixed up with something else. Mitch said she knew this woman in the middle of Saint Helier that would more than likely let you have her spare room. It's the one her twins slept in when they were little, but now they're in boarding school, it's empty. She doesn't charge much for it, and it's a bit kiddy-ish with trains on the walls; but clean and tidy.'

Stephen broke the intervening silence with one of his non-committal shrugs, and added a nonchalant smile,

'Sounds okay,' he said flatly, 'Where is it?'

She passed a crumpled piece of paper with an address scribbled on it in eyeliner, writing thick and crooked, but not quite black. Then she gave concise, clear directions as to how it could be found.

The woman who owned the place led us up to a train-spotter's paradise, and informed us that she'd bring toast and coffee in the morning. She hadn't time to prepare full breakfasts or evening meals. Too much faff, she'd said.

By the end of the holiday, Stephen was frustrated. He and Claire couldn't get down to the nitty-gritty, in either the hotel or boarding house, was constantly masturbating in the shower, and of the opinion that,

'I'd fuck a frog if I could stop it jumping.'

On our last night in Saint Helier, we had a drink with Claire, and her friends, at the hotel. Grolsch was served in porcelain, spring-loaded flip-top bottles, which everyone called *Flip Tops.* It was a hell of a lot stronger than the stuff they peddle as Grolsch now. It was dynamite.

We had four for starters, and bought two cases to put in the boot of the car to take home. We dropped the beer in the Ford, unsteady on our feet, as we headed into town, and ultimately into the garish, phosphorescent tentacles of the *Octopus* nightclub. Their warm embrace dragged us into the dark canyons of murky corners. Strangers lurked, loitered lecherously over drinks around the dance floor. It was the weirdest place I'd ever been in my life, but I was pie-eyed on Flip Tops.

A band was playing at one end of the cavernous club, and I vaguely remember shuffling over to the dance floor. People in front of the stage were cheering and applauding as I performed a jerky stop-start robot dance. The band was playing Gary Numan stuff, possibly *Cars*. I certainly didn't remember with any clarity what was going on. My memory only kicked in when I was walking to the rented room that night with Stephen, and Lena.

She was staggering between us, arm in arm. She bore an uncanny resemblance to Susan George, a popular actor at that time. She steered us on a detour, via a side street or two, and then invited us into her home for coffee. I was definitely in need of it if I'd been dancing, and Stephen would need it if he intended to satisfy his lustful cravings with this drop-dead-gorgeous young lady.

He was slobbering and drooling like a dog on heat, and when he was in that frame of mind, I knew he was determined to score. I sat in morose silence, listening to him plying silk-tongued techniques for seduction, sipping thick black coffee, and wondering if I knew the way back to my room on my own.

With a heavy sigh of resignation, I downed the bitter dregs of thick soupy coffee, carefully adopted a standing position, and said in a slurred, but dignified voice,

'Right, I'm heading off back now. G'night.'

Stephen was about to bid me a friendly adieu, with a predatory gleam in his eyes and wolfish grin on his face, but was silenced to slack-jawed stupidity when Lena told me to sit down, and stop being so obtuse. To add to his confusion, she turned to Stephen and said,

'Stop gawping and drink your coffee, mate, 'cos you need to be on your way home.'

I thought I was hallucinating. This couldn't be happening.

A woman was turning Stephen from her boudoir? A gorgeous young woman was telling him to be on his way? I was stupefied, almost to the point of speechlessness, and even more so when she put her delicate arm around my shoulder, pulling me closer to denim clad hips. She stated, oh-so matter-of-factly, that she wanted to find out exactly what made me tick; silent men were a mystery that Lena was fond of solving and, in a drunken stupor she mistook my drunken stupor to be a sophisticated silence. I didn't protest the point or argue as I waved smugly at Stephen's departing back.

I was awakened by warm naked flesh the following morning, not urging me to satisfy her passion, but for me to hide under the bed, as grandmother was about to enter the room. I slithered out from under the sheets, onto the lea of the bed, to slide in a serpentine fashion amongst the dust bunnies. I cursed the shag pile as it burned engorged genitalia with the friction as I did so. *I really need a piss. I hope this doesn't take long.*

Granny came up to remind Lena that she had to be at work by eight o'clock, and breakfast was almost ready. She was making scrambled egg - Lena's favourite, but she couldn't eat it when she was ill; once the tumours took hold. My stomach groaned at the thought of scrambled egg on toast, but I held hunger in check until granny had departed.

Lena thanked her grandmother, and assured her she'd be right down, but needed a quick shower first. The door had scarcely closed when she hissed under the bed for me to move my useless lazy arse and dress. Before I'd even half extricated myself from my hiding place, she was up and off to the bathroom, which she selfishly locked. I was standing in the middle of a room, completely buff naked, utterly gob-smacked at this turn of events.

I was sporting an uncomfortable erection, caused by a rising desperation to take a piss. *Fucking Flip Tops.* I didn't know what to do as I hopped from one leg to the other, but in the end, my desperation took over, and I'm ashamed to say that I sauntered to the bedroom window. *Yeah? You try a bit of sauntering with a fucking hard-on. I hobbled. I admit it.*

I watched in complete fascination, and rapture, as my erect, but slightly burned penis spurted a golden shower from the second floor window of a respectable middle-class house. Relief and ecstasy combined in one furtive act, watering beds of chrysanthemums and daisies below, with gay abandon on the equally respectable and middle-class island of Jersey. The icing on the cake was when I heard Lena's grandmother screech up the stairs that she might need her umbrella because it had started to shower.

Yeah, granny, it's pissing it down.

Lena returned to the bedroom, pink and naked from a shower, with only a towel wrapped around her head. I was reprimanded, with wagging finger and tongue, for still being there, and not sneaking down the stairs whilst I had the chance. I apologised, admiring her nakedness. She seemed completely oblivious to this fact, but then smiled disarmingly, sat on the edge of the bed to kiss me on the cheek. She told me how to get out of the house stealthily enough to avoid detection by granny, and to wait around the corner. Twenty-five minutes later, she hurtled around it so fast that she almost collided with me; flushed and excited, but radiant too.

'What did we do last night?' she asked, concerned.

'I don't know, I can't remember,' I answered.

'Did you fuck me?' more concerned.

'I don't think so.' I responded with more confidence, but also shocked by her candour.

'Good,' she smiled, 'I hate to fuck when I'm pissed or wasted. I prefer it when I'm sober, to be honest. That way I remember the ride better. Will you ring work for me this morning?'

'What do you want me to ring work for?' I asked.

'Well, you can tell them I'm sick, you know? Period pains, time of the month, and that sort of shit; women's troubles. Will you do it?'

'Yes, but why?'

She ignored this, and carried on regardless,

'Ask them if you can pick up my wages as well.'

I stood, staring at her in complete incomprehension.

'You will do it for me, won't you?'

A frown creased her perfect forehead, and then she added,

'Yeah?'

'I suppose so, yeah, but what's going on?'

'Busy day ahead,' she said flatly.

'Busy day?'

'Yep,' she beamed, 'you need to get me a ferry ticket to the mainland for the sailing tonight, and then we need to go back to my place to fuck. Are you up for it?'

'Ferry ticket?' I asked, ignoring the fuck completely, 'Why?'

'If you think I'm going to let a good-looking bloke like you sail out of my life without getting a few happy memories out of it, well, fat chance. Come on, let's find a phone box.'

I spent the rest of the morning finding my way back to the rented room, and explaining to Stephen about our extra passenger for the journey home.

He was gob-smacked at first, but then went into a fit of giggles over it,

'Stanley, you mad bastard, anybody else would take a stick of rock home, but not you. You're so weird.'

I went straight to the booking office for the ferry, and bought her a ticket, earning some strange looks from the lady who sold it, mainly due to me babbling inanely about why I needed a ticket in such an all-fired hurry. I raced back to Lena's, clutching the ticket firmly in a sweaty mitt. It was a warm day, and when I arrived at her home, I was lathered in perspiration, my clothing sodden, clinging to me, and my hair a matted mess plastered to my skull. The sight of a hot sweaty male seemed to send Lena into a passion that, up to this point, I had only read about, dreamed about, and probably fantasized about, but never actually encountered.

On the ferry, I silently endured Lena's carping about the lack of an available cabin where she could fuck my brains out. Other than her incessant desire to sleep, and snoring loudly in the car on the way up from Weymouth, it was a dull and trouble-free return.

The Escort drew to a halt outside my humble abode, bags were wrenched from the boot, along with a case of beer, and Lena followed me, in a bleary-eyed and sleepy stagger, to my parents' front door. We entered the house with a sheepishness that masked our infatuation for one another, performed the perfunctory introductions with the usual shyness and embarrassment. Then we made our way, heavily laden with baggage, up to an attic pied-à-terre to collapse exhausted on a newly made bed. We spooned on top of the duvet, arms clutching her, and cupping pert, firm breasts in my palm, letting sleep overtake us. We awoke in the early afternoon, refreshed but ravenous, made passionate love, before descending two flights of stairs to a dining room, and cooked a hearty fry-up, to be rinsed down with pots of steaming hot black coffee.

Bee was conceived that afternoon, and, although my parents weren't pleased by the news, they helped arrange a hasty wedding and reception at a local community hall. I found it quite ironic that Lena travelled all the way to Jersey, to get away from her brother, only six months before my holiday, but then return with me to have the family feud resolved; forgotten because of the imminent birth of a child. Michael even offered to be Godfather, but Lena declined. *Thank Christ.*

Looking back on those years, despite my anger, and the arguments over money, the worries about whether we were being good parents to Bee, I know they were good times. *Probably the best years of my life.*

I couldn't believe it when, after all the tests, scans and other crap they put her through, Doctor Smarmy told me she wasn't going to survive.

'In ten percent of cases, pancreatic cancer is inherited from the parents, symptoms confused with diabetes. Did your GP test her for diabetes, Stan?'

'I don't know,' I mumbled, 'I'm not sure.'

'Well,' he shook his head, 'it doesn't matter. Either way, it's not looking good. We could operate to remove the tumours, concentrate on chemo or radiotherapy, but, in the long term, we can offer little hope.'

I wanted to ram my fist into his fucking smug face at that point. I wanted to smash his head, like an egg, against the wall, watch brains dribble down pale blue emulsion. I wanted to shout in his ear,

'This is Lena you're talking about. This is the woman I've loved for almost thirty years; a beautiful woman who gave birth to my only daughter, and you're writing her off to let her die?'

I stormed out of the hospital, and never went back. I nursed Lena at home, fed her, cleaned her and, okay, there were times when I wanted to put a pillow over her face to end it for her, but I never stopped loving her.

I'm just disappointed that Bee never made it home to see her mother before she died, never came to the funeral, but I guess that hate is sometimes stronger than love.

I know my hatred of the Clampetts, and the mutt that bit me, might override my sense of loss. I hope so.

# Chapter Twenty-Two

I managed to access the Clampetts camera remotely, logging into their software using knowledge gained from watching the Wasp team. People tend to leave passwords set to default, and if not, it isn't rocket science to put the system back into it.

I've erased incriminating footage of me tossing an anti-freeze loaded tennis ball over the side fence at seven-thirty. Elly was applying make-up, getting ready for work or maybe on the phone to the taxi company. I don't care. Jethro won't be able to view it, won't see what happened, and that's fine by me.

I've removed the cuffs to let her dress.

'Have you wiped it?' Elly asks, pulling on a pair of Bee's flimsy panties, hooking the bra together at the front, sliding the clasp around to the back, looping straps over shoulders, and adjusting tits into cups.

'Yes, but I don't know what we're going to do about the messages, or the guys searching for you. Do you have any bright ideas?'

'I want to run, and keep running.'

'What about your son?' I ask, worried that she wants to bring him along, not that I know where we're going, or how we're going to get there. I couldn't see us getting far with a kid in tow.

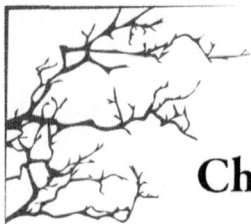

'He's with my sister now, so I'm not worried about him. They are animals but they would not harm a child.'

'I have my doubts about that, to be honest.'

I'm weighing up the options.

If I kill Elly, and bury her body under the pond today, who would know?

No-one. There's nothing to connect her to you, or the house now.

What if I let her live, and let her go?

Realistically? She's on the run from a bunch of pretty mean bastards. She owes them a lot of cash, has none of her own, so how far do you think she'd get?

Well, what if, suppose I visit the ATM at a local Post Office, draw some cash, let her go? What then?

How much will she need? Plus, if the Bulgarians do catch her, they'll take the cash, and if they don't kill her, they'll force her back on the game. Wait a minute,

'Were you working as a prostitute, lady?'

She looks away, embarrassed,

'Yes, sometimes, but also as unpaid cleaner, au pair, child minder and cook.'

'What about the hairdressing salon, near the church?'

'I work there from time to time, on appointment basis when ladies book in, but upstairs is a massage parlour and sex house, where people paid to fuck me.'

Great. I didn't really need to know that.

Well, you shouldn't have asked then, Stan.

'Did the owner know?'

She smoothes the red *Linkin Park* T-shirt over her tits, and tucks it into the waistband of blue jeans,

'Yes, the owner knew. Of course, they knew. They'd take ten percent of my money. Do you have any shoes for me?'

I look at her fake-tanned flippers with disdain,

'What size?'

'Thirty-eight-point-five,' she says.

'English size?'

'Oh, yes, six-and-a-half shoe, but seven in a trainer, if you have them? I prefer trainers.'

Fuck me, she thinks we're in New Look or Clarks.

'Wait here, I'll be back, okay?'

That sounded like Arnold Schwarzenegger.

'Okay,' she says, 'but hurry. Not much time.'

I bound up the cellar steps two at a time, then up to Bee's room, but her shoes are too small. Maybe Lena has a pair in that size. She was about as tall as Elly, so maybe they have similar sized feet. Lena never wore trainers, so she'll have to settle for shoes.

I can only find a pair of flat heels.

They'll have to do.

I'm halfway down the stairs when my phone pings with a trigger alert for the drive, and a dark shadow falls across the front door. I freeze, holding my breath.

Someone knocks on opaque glass, but I'm not sure if they'll be able to see me through it, lurking on the stairs, pretending not to be in. A hand is cupped to the frosted pane, a nose flattened against it as whoever it is peers in, rapping on woodwork once more. They must know I'm in, and they're not going away.

I'm hoping Elly stays put. I didn't have time to slap the cuffs on her, so I hope she doesn't decide to come up for a nosy around. There's an eager face pressing at the glass again, more hammering, and then a familiar voice shouts through the flap of the letterbox,

'Come on, Stan, open up. It's me, Glenda, and I want to play with Naughty Morty.'

Oh, fucking hell, Glenda, not now. Please not now.

# Chapter Twenty-Three

Glenda worked on the perfumery counter, and I was in the bedding and soft furnishings department. I liked my job, and found that working in soft furnishings helped me out with anger management. When I was in a black mood, or someone annoyed me, I could pummel a mattress, or kick the shit out of a sofa, to get it out of my system. We only started chatting one day when the canteen was full, and we were forced to share a table for lunch.

Most departments were preparing for the forthcoming Millennium, panicking in case computers crashed, or the banking system ground to a standstill or collapsed. I knew it was simply scare-mongering and Tommy-tosh, but you can't convince some people. Glenda was worried about it,

'I've started drawing cash from the bank each week, just in case things go pear-shaped,' she said, twirling a forkful of pasta.

I was tucking into a plate of sausage and mash, with thick onion gravy and peas. I frowned,

'Why would you do that? I mean, if things really do go wrong, I don't think a load of cash under the mattress would do you any good at all, you know?'

'Why not?'

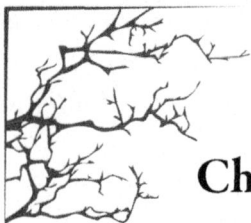

'Because,' I explained, 'if things go that wrong, then the marauding gangs who'll be out on the streets looting, pillaging and burning won't be interested in forming an orderly queue at checkouts to pay for goods, will they?'

'No, I s'pose not, but—'

'Your cash will be worth squat-diddley.'

'You really think so? I read somewhere that—'

'I wouldn't put too much stock in what you read in the papers, or hear on the gossip grapevine of television. This country depends too much on commerce to let it all slide down the toilet because of a date change.'

'Where do you work, by the way?' she asked, 'I've seen you a few times disappearing up the escalators.'

'Bedding and soft furnishings, and believe me, most of the idiots in that department are just that.'

'What?'

'Soft furnishings - without a brain-cell to call their own. Oxygen thieves.'

She giggled; a throaty, sexy sound - *dirty*, I thought.

It sent a shiver down my spine.

'I'm Stan, by the way,' I said holding out a hand over a gravy-stained plate.

'Glenda,' she replied, putting delicate, warm fingers into mine, 'Ooh, you have such big strong hands.'

'Thanks,' I said, 'although I'm not sure if it should be taken as a compliment or not.'

'Oh, it is,' she grinned, 'I like men with strong hands, and strong wills too.'

She seemed reluctant to let go of my hand, but finally broke the contact. I had the impression she was flirting.

You see, the thing is, before the Harvey Weinstein shit hit the fan, and #Me Too campaign, men and women in the workplace could flirt with one another, without the threat of a sexual harassment accusation being thrown at them. I mean, okay, there were dickheads who couldn't or wouldn't take no for an answer, pushed things too far, but they were in the minority, and they weren't only men. If I made a pass at a woman, and she made it plain she wasn't interested, then I'd move on. I wouldn't pester her.

Yes, I was a married man, but Lena drifted so deeply into a depression after Bee was born, that our sex life was non-existent, and, no matter how hard I tried - forgive the pun - I couldn't shake her out of it. I really did try to help her. I was patient and understanding, you know? Gave her the space I thought she needed, but nothing worked. Plus, we had a stroppy toddler to contend with, and Bee always needed feeding and changing, like a shit factory I guess, but she also required entertaining too.

I probably should have made Lena visit a doctor, and if I had, well, maybe he'd have picked up on her cancer quicker, but I'll never know for certain, and there's fuck-all I can do about it now.

Sitting opposite Glenda, and seeing mischief glinting in bright green eyes, sort of made me forget about Lena's problems, and Bee's moodiness. In fact, if I'm honest, I'd forgotten about Lena and Bee entirely, because I was too busy concentrating on Glenda's lips spreading into a wide smile,

'Yes,' she repeated, 'strong hands do it for me every time.'

I see a gold wedding band, diamond engagement ring below, and kind of pull back, mentally, you know? Think maybe I'd better not push my luck.

'How long have you been married?' I asked.

'Too long,' she said flatly, 'You?'

'I met and married my wife, Lena, in nineteen eighty-seven. She was pregnant with Lizabeth, so I guess you could say it was a shotgun wedding.'

'Well, I married in haste, and repented at leisure, but I seem to have a lot of leisure time to repent in.'

She sounded bitter, resentful, and sad too.

'Are things that bad?' I prompted, not expecting her to open up, because we'd only just met, but she told me the whole thing.

Her husband, Derek, was a nice enough bloke when they first met - he worked in insurance, but she didn't elaborate - intelligent and articulate, kind and considerate.

'He warned me that his work involved a lot of travel up and down the country, so I couldn't grumble when he did disappear for days on end. I shrugged my shoulders, spoke to him on the phone in the evenings at his hotel room, and looked forward to his return.'

I knew where this was going, or thought I did, but I was in for a surprise. You see, I thought that a guy on the road, up and down the motorways, sleeping in shitty dives like Travelodge, or the other one, Premier Inn; the one that smug fucker, Lenny Henry, is always pushing, well, he's bound to be lonely of an evening.

He could eat, have a drink, and watch television until he's so tired he'd nod off, and let the remote fall onto the floor. He could even jerk off in the shower if he was a bit horny, but ultimately the allure of flesh would get the better of him, the scent of a woman prove to much to resist, and he'd fall from grace, or for Grace. *Her name might not be Grace.*

'So, where did it go wrong?' I prodded, waiting for a tale of the other woman, and maybe another family living in a two-bedroomed semi in Cambridgeshire, maybe, but I get a totally unexpected bombshell.

'When he decided that dressing as a woman, picking up guys, and letting them fuck him, was better than being at home with me.'

'You're joking,' I said, but I could tell she wasn't. I mean, why would she?

'Nope,' she grinned, 'At first, I thought he was up to no good with some floozy from work, because I found a bra and panties, tucked into the lining of his suitcase. I wasn't snooping or anything, I came across them quite by accident.'

'Okay.'

'I challenged him, confronted him with them, and I expected the same thing I think you suspected, judging by the look on your face. That he'd tell me he was having a fling, or that he was shacked up with another wife, tucked away somewhere, maybe with a couple of kids, although I doubted that, because he always told me he didn't want them.'

'But, a transvestite?' I said, then realised I better keep my voice low, unless I wanted all the staff of John Lewis to know Glenda's marital secrets.

'To be honest, I don't know what he is, and for that matter, neither does he, but he begged me not to divorce him, not to leave, and said that, despite what I thought about his confession, he did love me.'

'He had a funny way of showing it, if you ask me.'

'Yes, well,' Glenda said, sighing, and sipping from a china cup, 'I eventually decided that sauce for the goose was also sauce for the gander.'

'You mean...?' I let that thought hang.

'Yeah, why not? If he can get his jollies picking up men in bars, then I see no reason why I can't do the same. I'm just more discrete about it, that's all.'

'So, he doesn't know?'

'He doesn't need to. He wasn't exactly forthcoming about his tendencies when we first met, or before we were married, so I see no reason to enlighten him now.'

'Oh. Okay,' I said.

Over the next few weeks, our meetings at lunchtime increased in frequency, became more honest, and overtly sexual, to the point where it was obvious Glenda wanted more than a sympathetic ear for her troubles.

She handed me a slip of paper with her address, and phone number on it, told me to use it, not lose it, and after a few text messages, we arranged to meet on our day off.

My fingers twitched as I fumbled the ignition key; hands shook as they hovered over the steering wheel, but then gripped it to begin the short drive. The Seat engine sputtered to life as I pressed hard on the pedal, gunning accelerator, eating up miles, weaving through slow traffic. I almost turned back several times, mind reeling with self-doubt, uncertainty over what I was about to do, but my over-riding desire was almost too much to bear.

I arrived at my destination, switched off the engine, looking furtively across to a rather plain, uninspiring two bedroom semi-detached house in the middle of an estate. As I climbed out of the car, butterflies tickling abdomen, I glanced around to make sure no-one was watching. I was on time, legs imitating jelly, and mind racing ahead.

I strolled past a blue Honda Civic, a tell-tale sign she was there and, for a moment, my fingers hesitated over a bell push. *Has she seen me arrive? Is she watching me now? Is she waiting on the other side of this flimsy door, eager and horny?'*

Once I pressed the button there was no turning back.

*I can't do this,* I decided, *it isn't fair on Lena or Bee,* but far too late, as my finger stabbed it, heard it chiming within.

The door opened and she stood, hands on hips, smile on her lips. High heels clattered on a tiled kitchen floor as she led me through a lounge to the bottom of the stairs. I followed closely as we ascended, boards creaking. She took a left into the bedroom. The curtains were shut, the bed made. Her arms snaked around my waist, pulling me to her.

'Let's play,' she whispered.

I wrapped a tie around her head twice, knotting it at the rear. I made sure it completely covered her eyes, but not too tightly.

'Ready?' I asked, enjoying the thrilling, but unbidden swelling, at my groin.

'Yes, Morty,' she murmured in submission.

Oh, Lord, the way she said that.

My hands looped around a narrow waist, unbuttoning a blouse from the top, pulling the tails free of the skirt when I reached the waistband, to let it fall from shoulders.

I unclasped her skirt, enjoying the sound the zipper made as I pulled it down, watching it gape wider before joining the blouse. She stepped out of the skirt, and I kicked the garments aside with a flick of a toe.

I was nervous, because I'd never done anything like this before, fingers trembling almost as much as she was, but I gazed in rapturous appreciation of her body. I kissed her shoulders, unhooked a lacy bra, dropping straps into the crook of arms, letting it slide effortlessly to the floor. I pressed closer, cupping and caressing breasts, palms grating over proud nipples, and peach smoothness of curves. She's aroused by the chill air on naked flesh, breath on her neck, and the bulge of my groin in the small of her back. Her head fell back onto my shoulder as I kissed her neck, nibbled her ear, hands exploring breasts, avoiding nipples, brushing or pinching them between thumb and forefinger, making her gasp in pain.

I ignored her gasps,

'Now,' I whispered, 'on the bed.'

Glenda stepped forward blindly, encountered the soft overhang of a duvet against her shins. She climbed onto the bed, shuffling until her back pressed against the cold metal of a head stand, pillows supporting her buttocks.

'Spread your arms for me,' I hissed in her ear.

She grasped brass uprights, as soft silk of a tie was drawn tight around her wrists, tethering her. I slid a flimsy lace thong along her thighs, past her knees and around her ankles. The thong dropped from her ankles over her high heels, as I applied subtle pressure at her knees, forcing them apart. She didn't resist. Her hips rose in response to my tongue teasing her labia, wanting me to probe deeper, make her cum. I stroked her legs, calves and inner thighs with the back of a hand; a soft delicate touch on her flesh, eliciting a moan,

'Oh, Morty, that's so naughty. Don't stop. Please.'

'Hush,' I said, pressing a finger to luscious lips.

I adjusted position, lowering my cock into her face, tempting her with it; she couldn't resist. Her lips parted, a tumescent shaft slid over an eager tongue, mouth clamped to engulf it. I pulled away. She moaned her frustration. My head was between her legs once more, lapping a clitoris relentlessly, driving her to the point of orgasm. Her hands grasped restraints as the first wave rippled over her body and she groaned, long and low in the back of her throat, spasms taking a deeper hold,

'Fuck me,' she begged through gritted teeth, 'Please, Morty, fuck me like a dirty slut.'

I stuffed the discarded thong in her mouth to silence her, and pinched her nipples, stroking her pussy with the head of my cock, thumb rubbing her clitoris, before I slid deep inside her. She squealed despite the makeshift gag in her mouth, hips thrashing wildly beneath me to meet my rhythmic thrusts. Her breathing a desperate panting as her orgasm rushed to the surface to overwhelm her. Hardness slid in and out like a piston as excitement mounted. She spat out the thong,

'That's it, Morty,' she hissed, 'fuck me. Please. Fuck your dirty slut-bitch, good and hard.'

# Chapter Twenty-Four

Well, that's that done and dusted, so to speak. It was hard work, dirty work too, but the body's in several pieces at the bottom of the hole, Postcrete in a cocoon around it, setting rock hard.

I actually wish John could have been here, but he's gone to the coast for the weekend, playing *Driving Miss Debbie* with Misery Tits. You see, if he'd been here, I'd have shown him the difference between a shovel and a spade.

A shovel makes a lovely *Spang* sound as it hits the back of a skull, reverberating a bit like a tuning fork, you know? Maybe more *Spoyoing* than *spang,* but either way, if I'd used the spade there would have been just a dull thud, with possibly a squelch. Beggars can't be choosers though; the shovel was the closest thing to hand at the time.

The spade is definitely the business when it comes to taking a head from shoulders, sliding effortlessly through tissue, although I needed to use a foot as leverage to drive it through vertebrae connecting it to the skull. *Crump!*

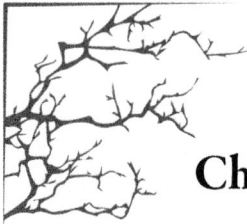

I was right about the hacksaw, and number of teeth per inch required; cutting through elbow and knee joints, ankles and wrists, like a hot knife through butter. I didn't count on it being so bloody messy - literally, and I wasn't sure about the torso. I'd read somewhere that bodies bloat and swell, but I'm not sure if that happens when they're encased in a thick layer of quick-setting concrete. I jabbed it a few times with the tines of a garden fork, to aerate it, like I used to do the lawns in September, before sprinkling grit and feed on it. I hope that will allow gas to seep away, and not disturb or distort the pond liner.

I used the shovel to mix more mortar for bedding the sandstone rocks around the perimeter, like Monty Don on *Gardeners' World*. I'm not sure if tap water is ideal to fill a new pond with, so I emptied the two large water butts, bucket by bucket, added some of the excess soil from the hole to form a bed for plants, and left it to settle. It took a couple of hours to move the rest of the soil up to the bottom of the garden using a wheelbarrow, and I was worried that the constant squeaking of the wheel may attract unwanted attention, especially after dark.

I needn't have worried. Tony was throwing a party in his back garden, with a lot of rowdy folk singing along to Tamla, getting drunk, and boogying the night away.

# Chapter Twenty-Five

It's my own fault really, because I know that, despite being hyper-charged when adrenalin is flowing, having my best ideas, thinking faster than ever, I can sometimes overlook things - obvious things - which is why I ended up in this fix.

I mean, dumping Elly's footwear on the way to the D.I.Y store was a good idea. I reasoned she wouldn't need them again, and they'd be evidence. Besides, flip-flops have always offended my sense of taste and decorum, and those crappy ones with a toe post, on what amounts to be little more than cardboard or thin plastic, are terrible. I'm irritated by folk shambling around supermarket aisles in clothing more suited to a beach; trunks and T-shirts, flip-flops. It's crazy.

Opening the door to Glenda wasn't the wisest choice I've ever made, or forgetting to cuff Elly to the pipe as I was hunting for shoes. I should have remained frozen to the spot on the stairs too, but no, I had to open it.

She squeezed in through the narrowest of cracks. I've mentioned how petite she is, haven't I? I'm sure I did. So, in she squirms, around the door, dressed in a mackintosh.

We're in the middle of one of the warmest driest summers on record, and she's wearing a mac?

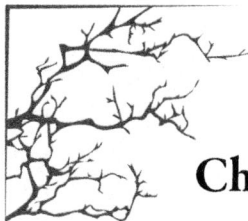

Yeah, she is, but other than a pair of stilettos, and a thong, she's wearing fuck-all else. The mac is cinched at the waist in a half-knot, which slides open as she pounces, pinning me to the stairs, moist warm mouth sealing mine. Her ripe breasts protrude; nipples proud, hard against my chest, as she fumbles with my belt buckle.

'Come on, Morty,' she gasps throatily, 'Bob's away, and it's time to play.'

I push her back,

'Not now, Glenda, please. I—'

'You know you want to—'

'We can't. I'm busy.'

She's hitching the thong off with one hand, the other tugging at buttons on my shirt.

I grab both wrists, glare into her eyes,

'I said no, Glenda.'

A sulky, sullen look spreads across her face, wiping any trace of lust away from sparkling green eyes. She sees Lena's shoes in my hand, frowns, and is about to ask me why I have them when Elly's scream echoes in the cellar.

'What's that?' Glenda asks.

'Nothing,' I say, trying to keep my voice even, but my mind is racing. *What the fuck's going on down there?*

She screams again, accompanied by the clatter of a chair hitting a stone floor.

'Stan?' Glenda asks, 'That was from your basement.'

I'm about to deny it, tell her she's mistaken, but then Elly bursts through the cellar door, eyes wild and wide,

'Rat!' she yells, 'There's a rat in the cellar!'

Okay, because there are woods at the bottom of the garden, sometimes, in the past, we've had the odd mouse venturing in, eating cereals in the kitchen cupboards, or nesting in the cellar, but never any rats.

Confusion reigns, bedlam erupts, as Elly and Glenda stand, face to face, in a babble of voices, in the hallway by my front door.

'Who's this? What's she doing here?'

'Please, Stan, there was a rat.'

'Why was she in your basement?'

'He killed my dog, kept me prisoner here.'

'Killed your dog? Prisoner?'

'Will you both be quiet!' I yell.

Silence descends.

'Glenda, meet Elly—' I start.

'My name's not Elly it's—'

'Never mind that now, Elly, this is Glenda.'

'My name's Maria,' Elly pouts petulantly.

Yes, and pretty soon, you'll find out how to solve a problem like Maria, lady.

'So, what's this about a dog, Stan? Why is she here, and what happened to her wrists?'

Blood is staining scruffy bandages.

'He kept me prisoner.'

'Prisoner?' Glenda almost shrieks, 'Why?'

I have to take control, and quickly.

'Look, let's calm down, sit in the lounge, shall we? I'll put the kettle on. We'll have a drink, and I can explain everything, okay?'

'He's going to kill me.'

Thanks, Elly.

'No, I'm not, Glenda. I changed my mind about that.'

'Oh, so you were going to kill her?'

'Look,' I sigh, 'let me explain, okay? This isn't what it looks like, or what you think. Trust me.'

Neither seems willing to do that, and exchange wary glances, but I pick up the shoes, hand them to Elly, then straighten my shirt and belt before leading them into the lounge. Instinctively, I draw the curtains together. I don't know why. The women sit on opposite sofas, eyeing each other with suspicion.

Fuck-fuck-fuckety-fuck-fuck-fuck, what a mess.

'Wait here,' I say, heading for the kitchen.

'He'll kill you too,' Elly assures Glenda, sliding fake tanned feet into flat heels.

'Elly!' I hiss, 'Let me explain it all, okay?'

As I'm waiting for water to boil, I start to tell Glenda about the Bulgarian Mafia, about the hair-dressing salon near the Mormon's church, about all the events at number seventeen, including slope-head, Prase, or whatever he's called. Elly interrupts, but I give her a warning glare,

'Let me tell her.'

'No,' Glenda says, 'let me see if I've got this straight, okay?'

'Fine,' I say, knowing Glenda has an obsession for detail.

'So, you were brought here, illegally, about eighteen months ago, by Bulgarian slave traders, yes?'

'Yes, with my son and sister—'

'They said you owed them the money for the journey, and then you were forced into prostitution to repay them?'

'Yes, Stan told you this.'

I nod, give her my *I-told-you-so* look.

She shrugs,

'Working at a salon that also doubles up as a brothel, or massage parlour, or whatever?'

Elly nods,

'Yes, plus sex parties, and other menial work.'

'So, why is she here in your cellar, Stan? Why does she think you killed her dog, and that you're going to kill her too?'

Elly looks at me with big blue eyes, and Stockholm kicks in again,

'Look, the dog attacked me, so I poisoned it, and then she came over here, dander up, and in no mood to talk to me rationally. She attacked me—'

'No, I didn't,' Elly protests, 'you pulled me into the house, put your hands over my mouth, grabbed my neck, and I passed out.'

I realise that from her perspective, maybe that's how things seemed to her, although I must admit to letting my anger get the better of me at the time.

'Is this true, Stan?' Glenda pushes.

'Sort of but—'

'And then you tied her up in the basement, ready to kill her?'

I can't deny it, so nod meekly,

'Yes, but that was before we, ah, shall we say, were, ah, better acquainted.'

Glenda looks at Elly, who says quite brazenly,

'Yes, we had sex, but I thought—'

'Oh, I know exactly what you thought,' Glenda says, 'you thought that if you had sex with Stan, he'd probably be less inclined to kill you, right?'

'Right,' Elly and I agree in unison.

The strange thing is, we're both laughing about it.

'Hmm,' Glenda says, 'I'd have done the same.'

'Really?' I say, surprised at the admission.

'Why not, Stan?'

Elly's phone rings again.

'Who is it?' I ask.

She hisses me to silence as she answers, to begin a heated conversation in Bulgarian for several minutes, and then severs the connection. I'm peeking through a gap in the curtains across to number seventeen, but there's no sign of activity.

'Prase is coming back to the house, and he says if I am not there when he arrives, I am a dead woman. They will find me, and they will kill me.'

'What about me? Do they know about me?'

Glenda thinks I'm motivated by self-preservation, and I suspect Elly may be thinking the same thing, but she shakes her head,

'No. But it won't take long for them to find out, and they will kill you too, Stan, because you have helped me to hide. We must run.'

'Okay,' I say, neurons firing like crazy as a ludicrous idea forms in the back of my mind, 'but I want you to do something first.'

'What?'

'Call your sister, tell her to take your son, meet us at the Mormon church.'

'That's awfully close to the salon,' Glenda says.

'I know, but it's a risk I'm prepared to take. Don't look at me like that. You'll see. I think this will work.'

I head for the stairs, up to the bedroom.

'What are you up to, Stan?' Glenda asks, puzzled.

'I told you. You'll see. Wait here.'

I thumb my phone to life as I climb the stairs, two at a time, heart hammering in my chest.

# Chapter Twenty-Six

Lena's chemo wig doesn't quite fit as well as I hoped it would, but it looks good enough. I think I prefer her as a honey-blonde to that shitty black dyed mess.

Glenda and Elly are staring at me as if I'm crazy, and maybe I am, but not crazy enough to let a bunch of thugs capture me, or kill me for that matter.

I hand Glenda a piece of paper,

'That's the address. Go straight there after her sister and the kid are safely aboard, okay?'

'Okay,' Glenda agrees, half-heartedly.

I really don't think her heart's in this.

'Glenda?' I prod.

'All right, pick up the kid and her sister at the church and drive them to this address. I've got it, although I'm not really dressed for it.'

'Whose fault's that?' I ask, but regret it.

'Never mind,' she grunts, 'we'll discuss this further when I'm back.'

'No.'

'What?' she bridles.

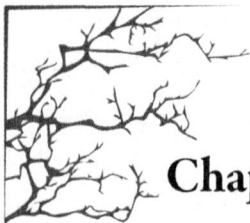

'No, Glenda, stick to the plan. Drop them off, drive home, and park the car on the drive. You push the keys through the letterbox, go straight home. Stay there until or unless I text otherwise, okay?'

'All right,' she agrees sullenly, 'Come on, Elly.'

'My name is Maria.'

'Well, come on Maria, let's get going.'

'Wait!' I say, a little too loudly, making them start.

'What?' they say in unison.

I open my wallet, and give Elly all the cash I have in there, maybe three hundred pounds, I'm not sure,

'Here, this should tide you over for a couple of days.'

She takes the money, folds it without counting it, and stuffs it into the front pocket of her jeans,

'Thanks,' she grins, 'I knew you were a kind man.'

'Oh,' I add, 'and no more selling your body, okay? You're free of that shit now. No going back. Promise?'

'I promise, Stan.'

I watch anxiously through the bay window, peering around a curtain as they climb into my Seat. Elly has arms full of shopping bags, although I don't suppose that will fool anyone. It was just an idea.

The car starts first time, but imitates a kangaroo as it bounces along the Cres, and Glenda becomes accustomed to the clutch.

# Chapter Twenty-Seven

Three-quarters of an hour later, my phone pings with a reassuring text message from Glenda;

'Arrived safe n sound. No probs. C.U. soon. X'

I send an immediate reply,

'Remind Elly to send the text to pig'

Glenda is on the ball,

'She knows. Chill.'

Okay, so far so good.

That's when my mistake comes back to bite me, with an alert on my phone, and a knock at the front door. I peer around a curtain to see Jethro on the step, waiting for me to answer. *He isn't supposed to be here yet. I'm not ready. Has Elly screwed up with the text messages? Fuck!*

What I don't realise is that I erased the footage of me throwing the poisoned tennis ball over the fence, but not footage of Ellie discovering the dead dog, and storming over the road, toward my house, shortly afterward.

I also wonder what happened to the dead mutt, but I have more pressing matters to attend to as the knocking recommences. I think Jethro is becoming impatient, but my car's not on the drive, so maybe he'll think I'm out, give it up, and go away.

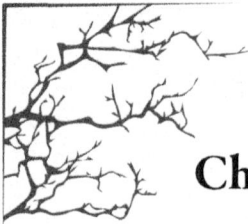

He might have too, if I hadn't taken a last peek, and let him see me.

Fuck!

I tap on the window, mouth the words, *back door*, my finger jabbing air toward the rear of the house. I see him jump from the step to saunter along the side of the house. My mind is doing summersaults as I try to think of a way to get rid of this chimp.

I open the door.

'Where is she?' he grunts, *like a pig*.

'Sorry?' I say, as though I know nothing.

'Where is Maria?'

'Maria?' I repeat like a dullard.

He holds up a phone to show me her picture.

I could try to bluff my way out, but I have a sneaking suspicion Jethro is on to me. I also think if I try to give him the run around, some more of his friends may join in the fun, and I don't want that. I don't want that at all.

I decide not to let this escalate, not to let him use the phone to summon the hellhounds.

'Oh, her,' I say, grinning like an imbecile.

'Where is she?' he repeats.

'She's, ah, hiding at the moment.'

'Hiding?' he repeats.

'Yes, hiding. Apparently, someone poisoned her dog and she thinks they're going to kill her, so she came over to me for help. I let her hide in my shed.'

'All this time? We have been searching for her.'

'Oh, well, sorry about that, but she didn't feel safe, so I let her stay.'

'In the shed?'

'Well, yes, but she's been fed, and there's a sink, and a tap in there. I use it as a sort of man cave. It has a small beer fridge too.'

'Show me. I want to see her.'

'Okay, follow me.'

I point to recent excavations,

'Watch your step around the hole there. I'm making a pond, so there's quite a lot of debris cluttering the place.'

He grunts, looks into the hole, as I knock on the shed door,

'Maria,' I coo through woodwork, 'someone's here to see you; a visitor.'

He barges me aside, yanking on the door handle, but the shed is locked, so he hammers on the door, and begins shouting her name. I panic in case someone hears him, but then remember John and Misery Tits are away, Tony will be at the kennels with Jules and the dog, and Bob is out of town. No-one will hear.

He lurches around to the window, cups a hand to peer through cobwebbed glass. *I must clean those windows.*

As he straightens, I slide a shovel from a pile of soil; hefting the handle to test the weight, swinging it around in a wide arc that ends with Jethro's skull as terminus.

The sound is delicious.

*"Come listen to my story bout a man named Jed"*

I hit him again, hard.

*"A poor mountaineer, barely kept his family fed"*

Another blow glances off a shoulder.

*"And then one day he was shootin' at some food"*

I deliver a final double-handed overhead smash to the skull.

*"And up through the ground come a-bubblin' crude"*

The last blow to his head is probably redundant, and I'm panting like a steam engine, but Jethro is dead.

*"Oil that is; Black gold, Texas tea"*

I drag him by his feet, down into the centre of the pit, unlock the shed to lift the first bag of Postcrete to the edge of the crater, ignoring the pinging of his phone. I know who it is.

# Chapter Twenty-Eight

I would have liked to go to Tony's for the party, but by the time I'm finished and showered, I'm all in and it's late, so with my trophy, Jethro's phone, and a couple of bottles of merlot, I sit in the back bedroom, fire up the computer, and set to work.

There are a few free online translation sites to choose from, so I experiment until I find one capable of making sense of the gibberish on Jethro's phone. Unlocking it was easy using the thumb I cut from the body with a pair of sharp secateurs - I just hope it's keyed to his right hand, and not his left.

I use the phone to completely wipe every last piece of footage from the camera's recorder at number seventeen, type in all the recent text messages, copying and pasting them into a Word document, before replying to several.

I make it clear that Elly is long gone, abducted by a rival Lithuanian gang, that Jethro isn't hanging around, in case they come for him, but don't bother waiting for any response.

I delete any photos of Elly, and all texts between her and Jethro, just to be on the safe side. Coppers are pretty dumb, but I don't want them getting lucky, and using the phone to trace her.

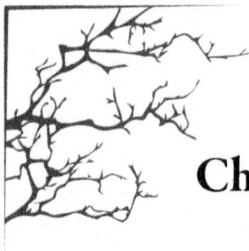

I use a detergent wipe to clean the phone thoroughly of any trace of my DNA, press the severed thumb to the button, and then drop it into a plastic bag. I also wipe the sealed plastic bag - can't be too careful about this. I pluck a pair of clean rubber gloves from under the sink and, although it's a bit of a fiddle and faff, put the phone into a jiffy bag, then return to the computer.

I type up the relevant information, print it off, along with a label, addressed to the nearest police station, stick it to the jiffy, and seal the bag.

I head down into the lounge, fire up the television to watch my version of *Match of the Day* - a replay of the death of Jethro in my back garden. It's fascinating stuff; zooming in for a close-up of the shock on his face as I hit him with the shovel, a body twisting to face me as the second blow impacts. It's kind of cathartic to see. I even groan in disappointment as the third blow is deflected to bounce from a shoulder, making me topple slightly, and have to readjust my position as he crumples to the floor.

I think the best bit though, is the look of pure hatred on my face as I deliver the last double-handed overhead strike. I watch that part a dozen times in glorious slow motion before letting normal viewing speed resume.

The burial and tidying up are pretty lacklustre, and a bit tedious to sit through, but I want to make sure I didn't miss anything, left no stone unturned so to speak.

The second bottle of merlot relaxes me, puts me in a mellow mood, and I wonder how Elly is doing, how she's settling in at the new place. I'm almost tempted to send her a message, but glance at the clock, and think better of it. *I'll check on her tomorrow.*

I take one last look at the murder before wiping the footage from the hard drive, finish the wine, and turn in for the night.

The following morning, I notice the Navara on the drive at seventeen, but there's no sign of Baldy, although the Meathead minibus driver is shambling around in the back garden. I don't know what they're up to, or care. Maybe they're cleaning the place, getting it ready for the next woman and her minder, or looking for a clue as to where Jethro may have gone. I put on a fresh pair of thin rubber gloves, and a coat, stroll to the post office for stamps. They sell self-adhesive things now, so I won't have to lick them, and give police my DNA. The woman at the counter weighs the package, asks me how valuable it is, if I want to send it recorded delivery, and I know that if I opt for any of those, I'll have to put my information on the jiffy bag label.

Fat chance.

'No thanks,' I say cheerily, 'I only wanted to know how much it would cost to send it second class parcel.'

She ignores the gloves, tells me that if I post it now, it will arrive no later than Thursday morning.

'No, that's okay,' I reply, 'I'll take the stamps for it, and post it when I've contacted the recipient, thanks.'

'Are you sure?' she presses.

'Quite sure, thanks,' I grin, 'I don't know when they need it by, to be honest, so I'd better check.'

She hands over the stamps, takes my cash, and I walk further along the road to a branch of *Ladbrokes*, use a free counter to peel the stamps onto the bag without touching them - again a bit fiddly - before returning to the post box, and dropping it into the slot.

Last collection: 1700? That'll do me.

# Chapter Twenty-Nine

I'm with Tony, drinking in what used to be my local, before I moved to a one-bedroom flat on the outskirts of town, and put the house on the market.

I was riddled with guilt about leaving Lena's ashes at first, although I reasoned that after a deluge, and Baldy's piss, there'd be precious little left anyway.

It doesn't matter now, I told myself, I still have all those wonderful memories of the good times we had.

Glenda tried to rekindle things with me once the shit died down, and Elly was safe, but I decided that I'd prefer to move on with my life, not re-visit the past, well, aside from Lena that is. She took it reasonably well, all things considered.

The estate agents were impressed by the back garden, particularly the pond, which I'd spent a few days planting up with various marginal and deep water specimens, and I told them about the newts too.

Okay, they're fictitious newts at the moment, but I'm fairly sure that by next summer, there will be newts. It's a bit like that Kevin Costner movie from 1989. You know the one? *Field of Dreams*. It's the one where a ghostly voice whispers to him,

"If you build it, he will come"

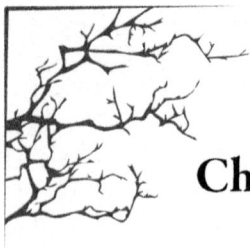

Well, I built it, and I reckon they'll come, and, as the newts are a protected species, new owners must be made aware of this fact, and not dig it up.

'Oh, no, Mister Mortimer,' the rep grinned, 'the pond is a really excellent feature, and a strong selling point. I'm sure no-one would want to rip it out, it's lovely.'

I've had a couple of nibbles, if you'll pardon the pun, from prospective buyers, and I'm surprised at how much the place has increased in value over the years. It will net me quite a handsome sum when it's sold.

Tony takes a sip of Guinness, pulls a sour face,

'You did the right thing moving out, Stan, my man. The fucking Pikeys are still at seventeen, but I've not seen the highway maintenance guy since you left.'

'Really?' I say.

'Yeah, the big bald-headed twat and the minibus man are there now, but I've seen a couple of women too.'

Maybe the cops never received the phone I sent.

'How's Elly doing at the kennels?' I ask, changing the subject.

'She's settled in fine, man; running the show like a pro.'

I raise an eyebrow, and give him a look.

'Yeah, I'm sorry about that. I forgot. She found the kid a good school and her sister is helping out running the business too. I'll be sorry to see them go to be honest.'

'Go? Go where?'

'Well, she says she's going to save up enough cash to fly home and move in with her folks in Bulgaria. Oh, that reminds me—'

Tony pulls out his wallet, peels a wad of notes from a back compartment, and hands them over,

'Maria asked me to give you this.'

'What is it?'

'It's the money you lent her, remember?'

'No, I gave it to her, Tony. Give it back to her.'

'No way, man; she says you have to take it, and I'm to pass on her thanks, so there it is. Thanks, Stan.'

'But—'

'No buts, put it in your pocket, buy a few beers with it. It's your round, by the way, man.'

I head for the bar, mulling things over. I buy Tina a Bacardi and coke, slide a pack of dry-roasted nuts into my back pocket, and rejoin Tony at the table.

The dog hears the rustle of the packet, looks up at me with a daft expectant expression, licking her lips.

'No, Trixie,' Tony says, 'lay down, girl. Good dog.'

'Have the police ever been to number seventeen?'

'Not that I know, man. Why'd you ask?'

'Just curious, that's all.'

'A new couple have moved into number nineteen.'

'Oh, what are they like? Noisy?'

'Nosey more like. A young couple; might be married, but I'm not sure, man. They're always at the windows, day and night, peering around the curtains, watching who comes and goes, you know? Like a neighbourhood watch only more intense. Creepy if you ask me.'

'Yeah,' I agree, 'Creepy.'

I have a few more beers, make my excuses and toddle off to catch my last bus home, thinking about new people in number nineteen, and what Tony said.

Maybe the cops did receive the phone, after all, and maybe number seventeen is under surveillance now. I'll keep my eyes peeled on the local press, just in case.

# Chapter Thirty

I had a letter from Elly, postmarked Bulgaria, but I haven't the foggiest idea as to how she found my address. Maybe Tony gave it her, but it's an open invitation to visit for a holiday, to stay with her, and her folks, in Sofia. It's tucked in the inside pocket of my jacket, and I'll read it again once I'm through the airport security checks, and on the aircraft.

Other than my jaunt to Jersey, I've never been out of the country, and getting a passport, buying tickets, and all the fuss and palaver involved were a challenge. Still, it's over, and with cash from the sale of the house, I should be set for my new life abroad.

I'm apprehensive about what the kid will think of me, you know? He doesn't know me from Adam, and it could be awkward at first, but I'll have to try to win him over as best I can. The language may prove to be a bit of a barrier at first too, but I'm pretty quick on the uptake when it comes to that kind of thing. It must be easier than learning Japanese, and I did that.

I was irritated by the queues of people at the airport concourse, but I didn't let the old angry Stan take over. I put that cantankerous cancer in the ground when I buried Jethro, and I've managed to keep a lid on my temper ever since.

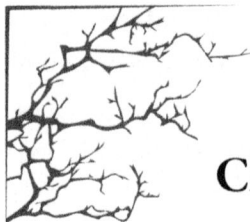

Relaxing on the plane, I read Elly's letter again, have a contented glow in the pit of my stomach knowing that she's safe, away from any possible harm, but have a fit of giggles when I think back to my last conversation with Tony.

'He's still missing, you know,' Tony said.

'Who?'

'Maria's bloke, what's his name?'

'I used to call him Jethro, she called him pig.'

'Yeah, well he disappeared just after Maria took over at the kennels, which I thought was weird, but hey, man.'

'Maybe,' I said with a wry smile, 'he sleeps with the fishes, Tony, eh?' *Or the newts.*

I'm pushed into my seat at take-off, relishing g-force compressing my chest, setting off for my new life. It's a long flight and, at the end of it, I've fences to mend, and bridges to build, but I'm hoping Bee will understand.

I guess my first meal in Canada will be humble pie.

We'll see.

# After Words

My thanks for reading this story, in whatever format that may be, and I sincerely hope that it gave you as much pleasure to do so, as it did for me to write.

Feedback and criticism are always welcome, whether good or bad, because both are positive to a writer.

Pointing out where we do badly is as important as praise for what we do properly, and we learn from both.

We strive to improve, to better ourselves, to make the writing and reading experiences more enjoyable.

So, I ask one last small favour of you before you go, and I return to my next tale of misery and woe. Please be so kind as to leave some feedback, wherever you obtained a copy of this book, to let both myself, and others, know your thoughts about this particular story. Reviews take so little time to write and are always appreciated.

Thank you.

# Teasers

# Robert Machin

The pedestrian precinct is normally bustling; a place full of busy people, dashing purposefully in and out of shops, determined to go about their business, in spite of the crush. Today, however, the weather's deterring many; drizzle and blustery winds whip water around pavements, or lash it against store fronts.

Robert scowls at slate grey heavens, drops a rucksack at his usual pitch, and unpacks magazines. He prefers to stand outside an arcade entrance to the main shopping complex because that way he can catch the eye of people entering or leaving, and hopefully raise more money.

He has at least prepared for lousy conditions today by putting on an extra layer of clothing under a scruffy parka jacket, wrapping hands snugly in grey, fingerless woollen gloves, and putting on his old faithful woollen cap to keep out the chill. Penetrating rain is something he hasn't factored in and knows that, by lunchtime, he'll be soaked to the bones. Damp is already creeping through the soles of trainers, and soaking cuffs of trousers.

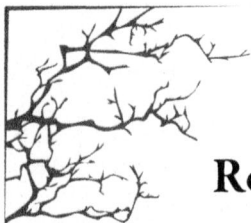

He hates rain more than snow. Cold nights sleeping rough on the street are better than miserable wet ones, when bedding and clothing are damp and clammy for days after a downpour, and nowhere to dry them properly. They cling to skin, making it nigh-on impossible to have a good night's sleep.

He longs for summer; warm, long days when people are happier, more liable to toss a few extra coins his way, particularly after they sink a beer or two in nearby pubs. His mouth waters at the thought of alcohol. It's been a long time since his last bender, and knows that if he takes one sip of amber nectar, he won't so much fall off the wagon, but actually take a full-blown leap. He hums the hook line of an old Lena Martell recording of the song *One Day at a Time* to get it out of his mind,

"Lord, help me today. Show me the way. One day at a time."

Another wild gust of heavy rain lashes his parka like shrapnel, wind whips the hood from his head and there's the piercing sting of water droplets against his cheeks. They cling to a ragged beard, grey and tangled, as he pulls magazines from the safety of a rucksack. There's little point in spreading them out, as they'll only end up being an irretrievable mush, so he leaves a half dozen on top of the sack as sacrifice to a god of inclement weather. He covers them as best he can, using a plastic bag to keep them dry, but fighting a losing battle. Ninety-five percent of shoppers will completely ignore him, and walk past as if he's a ghost, or doesn't exist.

They'll deliberately choose not to see him.

Of the other five percent, three might oblige him and buy a copy, perhaps add extra coins to the selling price, netting him the price of a hot chocolate, and there'll be no problem. He'll thank them politely; tug his woollen cap, and smile. He'll bid them a Merry Christmas, or a Happy Easter, or whatever pointless festival is happening at that time of year, or sometimes simply, 'Have a pleasant day'. It costs nothing to be sociable or polite.

The final two percent are the ones he hates most.

Evenly divided between nosey well-wishers - who'll only part with cash if he details his fall from grace - or abusive arseholes - who have no intention of parting with money, no matter what the cause. The nosey ones will interrogate him until he tells them why he's a down and out, how he's squandered opportunities in life. He hates them because he can see pity lurking in their eyes, and the mewling sympathetic noises they make as he tells them turns his belly, makes anger rise unbidden.

Abusers are obvious to spot. They announce intent by body language. Robert's become adept at deciphering the code of people's body language. He can spot the subtle twitch of a hand that will soon be reaching for a purse or a wallet, the look in the eyes that tells him money will be forthcoming. The slight deviation from an intended path which would take them scurrying past into the sanctuary of the shops makes it clear they're going to give him the last of their spare change.

Some will buy hot drinks on punishingly cold days, or soup if he's lucky, and once, a kind old lady dragged him by the elbow into a patisserie to buy him a pot of Earl Grey tea and a buttered scone. Of course, in return for her kindness, she wanted to know his life story, but he didn't begrudge her his tale. The more he tells it, the less it remains his life; gradually distancing himself from the bad things that happened over the years, coming to terms with the painful and acrimonious split from Lorna and the girls, a headlong leap into insolvency, alcoholism, and his ultimate homelessness.

One day he might come to terms with their deaths.

Thinking about it hurts, and he needs to change the subject, take his mind off it. It isn't healthy.

He ignores the rain for a moment; lets the magazine nestle into the crook of an arm to begin a mental chant. The rhythm spreads from mind to body. Two small bounces on his left foot, and two on his right, letting legs sag slightly at the knee to keep his balance. It's a song he heard a few years ago, when he used to have a better pitch outside a local HMV branch, before it closed down to become another McDonalds.

People are hungry for nostalgia, and music from the seventies or early eighties is being re-discovered by the next generation. He summons up the driving rhythm, and lets his feet move in time to the inner beat,

"It was one of those nights when you turn out the lights and everything comes into view."

Socks squelch inside trainers as he hops from one leg to the other, cold moisture oozing between toes, over the top of his feet, then sucked back as he lowers them to the ground. Trouser-cuffs slap on pavement slabs; blotting puddles of rain to soak calf muscles, where material clings to flesh. Incessant rivulets drip from the hem of his parka onto the crotch of pants; freezing genitalia, making him numb from the waist down. He desperately hopes that tonight there'll be a spare bed for him at a hostel and, if he's early, enough hot water for a bath before supper.

He's into his stride, music blotting out memories, focusing on the job at hand, as the gravelly voice of Bon Scott, AC/DC's lead singer, croons in his head,

"She had a touch. A touch too much."

He straightens a plastic identity badge, pushes the magazine further along his forearm, adjusting the weight, and his grip, to begin his daily ritual. His lips parting in a friendly smile as he shouts relentlessly,

'*Big Issue.* Get your *Big Issue.* Come on, people; get your copy of the *Big Issue*.'

As he watches a seemingly endless stream of grim, disinterested faces passing by for the comfort and warmth of the shops, he tries not to concentrate too much on the date. He wants to ignore the significance of it, to quash all trace of the memory of what today means to him.

His dance remains uninterrupted, as does the singing inside his cranium, but he knows he cannot erase facts. He thinks of Lorna, Alex and Bev, swallows past a lump in his throat. Sudden constriction of the oesophagus in reflex to mental stimuli hurts so much he cannot bear it.

If any of the grim, determined faces heading for the shopping centre looks closely at the filthy, dishevelled homeless man peddling copies of the *Big Issue*, they'll see teardrops, forced from his eyes, running down his cheeks, mingling with rain to gather in his beard.

# Drain

The rat floats along sluggish waterways, not quite dead, but lacking strength to climb out, surrendering to slow-moving currents. It tumbles over a weir, rolling on rough stones, sliding onto the slipway, through a slime-coated incline to drop into a stagnant pool. It lies for several days, waiting for pain in its shoulder and head to subside. It can no longer see out of one eye. A lead pellet shattered the orb, whistling through the skull, narrowly missing the brain. Hobbling along, searching for food, regularly attacked by other vermin, it eventually finds sanctuary amongst a raft of wet-wipes, cotton buds, soggy take-away wrappers, and an encysted amoeba, *Naegleria Fowleri*.

The ten-micron diameter ball possesses no brain, no desire, and no preferences. It's incapable of thought; its sole purpose is feeding and reproducing. It was washed from the security and warmth of a bacteria-laden pond, behind an abandoned factory, during a clean-up operation by the council, preparing ground for bulldozers to move in.

Scraps of greasy fat-rich food cling to paper, so the rat eats enough to remain alive for a few more days.

The amoeba changes from cyst to trophozoite phase, gorging, multiplying around the rodent, extending several cell membranes filled with plasma to enable locomotion, and the ability to spread.

At the onset of a bitter January winter, temperatures plummet, freezing water around the rat, trapping corpse and amoeba in ice, until a thaw and heavy rain wash the raft into the Fleet. It swirls in random eddies, gathering detritus, enveloping the body in a coating of congealed oil and solidified fats, slowing its decay, preserving and mummifying the dead animal, providing the amoeba with an ideal medium for reproduction.

# Fires

Bedlam erupts at a house on Umgeni Road, and Fires drifts in and out of consciousness, floating on an ocean of agony; battered and bleeding, as he lies amidst wreckage of the fruit stall.

The choking stench of smoke, crackle of flames and flickering shadows of neighbours intrude upon the pain. Shards of glass and timber splinters, deeply embedded in his flesh, make it almost impossible to lay still, but eager hands press warm blankets around his nakedness.

Reassuring voices murmur to him.

'Stay there,' someone says, 'help is on the way.'

'He jumped from a window to escape the fire,' a man states.

'What about Mohanlal and Mohinder?' another asks, accompanied by the sound of sheets being torn into strips.

'They're trapped inside,' is the shocked response.

'Can we rescue them?' a concerned male voice asks.

'No, the flames are too intense. Will he live?'

Fires finds it difficult to focus on their faces in the darkness.

'The local fire crews will be here soon.'

'What about a doctor? Has anyone summoned a doctor?'

'Suhani is searching for him.'

Fragments of memory replay as a cool hand is placed on his forehead; a reassuring voice implores him not to move. Searing white heat fills his groin where someone kicked his balls and, as he writhes on the floor, another man hauls Mohinder into the air; impaled on a vicious blade.

'Mohinder is dead,' Fires mumbles.

'Hush,' a woman hisses.

'Mohanlal,' he slurs, 'dead too.'

'Be quiet, help is on the way.'

'Too late,' Fires says, 'too late.'

His left arm is stinging, pounding where blood seeps from a gaping knife wound, his right arm a dead weight by his side; his right thigh, groin and stomach burn and throb.

The window, he realises, I went through the window.

Seconds of weightlessness and the dizzying sensation of twisting in mid-air, turning and falling, bracing for the imminent impact, come rushing back. The crack of dried timbers collapsing beneath him, the smell of fruit and vegetables, and the bone-jarring cold of stone cobbles as his head strikes them becomes reality once more.

'I went through the window,' he whispers, as mind and body shut down, surrendering to shock.

Fires languishes in a bed at Addington Hospital for several weeks after, attended by Doctor William Addison, a sprightly surgeon in his mid-fifties. He's stick thin, with a corona of unruly white hair; skin the texture of puckered leather. Fires is angered by the fact that there was no investigation by the authorities into the deaths of two Indians. No foul play was discovered or suspected.

'Does no-one care?' he wails to the doctor.

'They killed my family,' he tells nurses, 'why will no-one believe me?'

Ghandi is stirring up all kinds of mischief and Indians are viewed as being almost as bad as kaffirs.

He's frustrated by the indifference shown when he recounts his version of events, and becomes furious when they decide the fire started in the kitchen area; caused by an upturned kerosene lamp. The attending fire crew decide the Indians were overcome by fumes and perished in the blaze. No-one noticed or questioned the obvious knife wounds on their burned and blackened flesh.

To add to his misery, Fires discovers a funeral was held for Mohanlal and Mohinder in his absence; their charred remains ceremoniously placed in the sealed back room of a neighbour's house, facing south, with an oil lamp burning at their feet for three days. The corpses were bathed with purified water, dressed in new clothing, and taken to the river's edge by a few mourners; paid for by the solicitor from money left in the Valjee estate.

Ironically, their desiccated husks were cremated in the traditional Sikh ceremony of Antam Sanskaar.

Bill Addison is standing at the foot of the bed, bright blue eyes peering at Fires over the rim of his pinc-nez spectacles,

'I'm worried about you, young man,' he says, 'extremely worried, to be honest.'

Fires averts his gaze. He knows Bill and the nursing staff are concerned for him. Physically he's mending quickly, but his mental state seems fragile, especially during waking moments when he sits and stares beyond the foot of his bed at a void none of them can peer into, or comprehend. There seems little they can do to help. He's lost to them, communing regularly with the ghost of Marietta Rensburg; a girl from a mass grave at Pinetown.

'God will not forgive you,' she murmurs, as maggots writhe over her lips, tumbling from her tongue.

'No-one will forgive me,' he responds, 'and my sins will always haunt me.'

'Always,' she hisses in agreement.

Her black-eyed glassy stare is hypnotic, but Bill's voice intrudes, breaking the spell.

'You have to let it go, Fires. Please,' Bill says, not bothering to mask increasing exasperation at the young man's obsession, 'it's not good for you.'

Fires glares back at him,

'Forget about it, eh?'

'There's nothing you can do.'

'So, I simply accept the fact that my family were murdered?'

Bill shakes his head,

'You can't prove that, Fires.'

Wincing at the pain it causes, he flings back sheets, points at stitched wounds,

'Where did these knife wounds come from, doctor? Answer me that if you can?'

'Those lacerations,' Bill intones with solemnity, 'are consistent with those inflicted by someone leaping from an upstairs window.'

'Fok jou!' Fires spits, wrapping the covers around his torso.

'And,' Bill continues, ignoring the expletive, 'you fell from a considerable height, sustaining a severe head trauma.'

'Oh, yes,' Fires hisses, voice filled with sarcasm, 'the boerkie boy banged his head, and doesn't remember a single thing that happened to him?'

Bill sighs, shuffles papers for a moment, marshals his thoughts and then speaks,

'Grief, and guilt often play tricks on one's mind.'

'What are you implying, Bill?'

'Nothing, I'm implying nothing.'

'Then what? What are you saying?'

'I'm saying that, given sufficient time to rest and recuperate; you may have different recollections of the events of that night.'

Fires' response is sullen, waving the doctor away with an impatient hand,

'Go, Bill. Please, just go.'

He watches the white coat flapping, billowing behind him as Bill leaves the ward, shaking his head and running a hand through the shock of white hair atop it; frustration personified.

Ignoring a stabbing reminder by a broken collar bone, Fires lies back, closing his eyes to wallow in memories of a middle-class life in Bombay; adopted son of Mohanlal Valjee, brother of Mohinder, knowing that it was ripped away from him, and that only ghosts remain.

As he's nursed back to health, letting his broken body mend, stitched wounds knit together to give way to scabs and ultimately puckered scars, Fires' mind replays events of that night. Over and over they unfolded before him, in a seamless but endless stream of confused and distorted images. Sometimes they become interwoven with the deaths of mother and father, or a long and painful journey from Pretoria to Durban.

Shivering, as he trudges through biting cold, trekking on the veldt, gazing up at the moon or the stars for a bearing. Sweating, as he tries to sleep during the day, constantly wary of discovery by marauding troops, plagued by flies, and the guilty relish of savouring human flesh to sustain him. Animated cadavers chase him; taunt him, as waxy flesh melts from bones, or splits with putrefaction, allowing maggots to tumble from their haven.

And I will never forgive you, Marietta echoes.

A nightly mishmash of horror and sorrow rob him of sleep, tossing and turning in a cot, crying out in anguish with pitiful regularity during his confinement. Then, one night, as a summer thunderstorm rages outside his window, he's looking out onto The Point by the harbour and ocean beyond, with skies that are black and baleful; leaden, sundered by forks of fierce lightning.

He wraps his body in mental armour, forged from pure hatred, letting a banner of vengeance drape around his shoulders and stuffing remorse and sorrow into a dead zone he creates within. He summons up a mantra to sustain him in his thirst for revenge, taken from the teachings of the Indians who adopted him, which he subtly alters to suit his desires:

'Now I am become Death, the destroyer of worlds, and I will have my vengeance.'

He awakes refreshed as morning sunlight filters in through a window by his bed, casting long shadows over a ceiling of the ward, and he smiles. The smile broadens into a wolfish, predatory grin at memories of the previous night, and the decision he's made. He will not be deflected from his goal. Nothing will stand in his way. He hungers for revenge.

# Stephen

March usually announces its arrival with lion's roar, departure a lamb's bleat, but the reverse is true this year. Wind and driving rain swirl in Grove Park Cemetery, as he watches from a shelter of overhanging trees. He peers from behind evergreen shrubbery, masking his presence. Mourners huddle around an open grave. Bullets of water lash flesh, soaking clothing, as he stands dispassionate, attention fixed on the gathering.

One by one, he picks out familiar faces, some tearful, clutching tissue to red-rimmed eyes, others sombre, stern; ashen faces, vision glazed. Jacqueline Latham, George's first wife, and Stephen's biological mother, is supported by husband, Mike, standing close, arm around a shoulder to comfort her. She's sobbing uncontrollably, auburn hair limp, bedraggled, as it cascades over hitching shoulders. Sarah, Stephen's stepmother, sways as if on the verge of a faint. Danny Bullock puts an arm around a narrow waist to comfort her, pulls her upright to steady her; two of Stephen's former lovers, side by side, bearing witness to his interment, a final resting place in the family plot.

*How ironic,* he muses, *and so touching.*

He sets his jaw against a desire to laugh, watching as another of Stephen's former lovers, Andy, inhales deeply, scowling at grim leaden skies full of thunder, tanned face spattered by a downpour soaking an expensive suit.

*If their sins and peccadilloes were laid bare, oh, my, how the tears would really flow.*

He ignored the chapel service prior to the burial, not wishing to hear the snot-nosed whining; the snivelling and sycophantic ramblings of a priest who knows little about Stephen Mangham, cares less about his life, or his tragic death no doubt. Nor did he wish to endure endless streams of redundant platitudes, eulogies or associated religious mumbo-jumbo for the dead,

'I am the resurrection and the life, sayeth the Lord; he that believeth in me, though he were dead, yet shall he live: and whosoever liveth and believeth in me shall never die. I know that my redeemer liveth.'

A wry chuckle will not be subdued,

*Amen to that, Amen indeed.*

Memory is stopped short as he sees the final face by the graveside. George Mangham, wheelchair resting on a hastily constructed timber platform to prevent sinking in mud and mire, tartan blanket covering thighs and knees against the chill. Immaculate black jacket, white shirt and black tie, soaked, but smart as ever; George is the only mourner, besides Mike Latham, who holds no love in his heart for Stephen, his son. In fact, George sees Stephen as nothing but an agonising failure, both as a child and as an adult, cause of a recent stroke and myocardial infarction leading to his current incapacity.

The priest is coming to a close,

'We therefore commit Stephen's body to the ground, earth to earth, ashes to ashes, dust to dust; in the sure and certain hope of the resurrection to eternal life.'

Roses are thrown into the pit, cloying clay rattles on a coffin lid as handfuls are tossed down, and George, face set in stony mask of indifference, shakes his head. Eyes fix on shrubbery, peer under overhanging branches to see the silhouette of a stranger standing in shadow. Eyes lock with George's unflinching gaze, and he swallows past a constriction in a dry throat. They know the truth; realise what the other hides.

George's hand slides from under tartan, skeletal and pallid, finger extended, thumb raised like the hammer of a gun, pointing straight at him. He smiles, shrugs off the old man's threat, pushes hands deeper into warm pockets of an overcoat to stride away. The entourage turns, headed for welcome sanctuary in sleek black limousines parked at the rear of a hearse, eager to be out of the wet.

George watches the departing figure of the man in the overcoat, strolling over carefully manicured lawn, around flowerbeds of vibrant wind-blown spring colour, between monuments to mortality and stone statuary toward an exit.

By the time George is bundled into a car, wheelchair stashed in the boot, the man is long gone, and George is unable to spot him on a slow drive back to the Mangham residence for a meal, but he is watching the cortege.

He is watching and waiting, biding his time, until he knows the moment is right.

Then he will strike.

Then he will right all their terrible wrongs.

*Yes. Vengeance is mine, sayeth the Lord, and I shall repay.*

Printed in Great Britain
by Amazon

46986973R00099